"I TOLD YOU TO TAKE THAT SHIRT OFF."

"You'd use any excuse, wouldn't you?" she snapped, wriggling one arm out of the shirt, then the other, wincing slightly as he lifted the garment away from her bruised back. Skye half-sat on the edge of the bed and began to apply the ointment. Her skin was smooth, soft, exciting to touch, and he had to force himself to keep his mind on the task.

"It works quickly. You'll feel better soon."

"I'm feeling better already, all warm and kind of tingly," she said as her arms encircled his neck. "Thanks," she murmured, her lips pressing against his mouth.

"Just saying thanks?" he asked.

She half-shrugged. "There's thanking and there's wanting. I don't know where one starts and the other stops . . ."

NAL BOOKS ARE AVAILABLE AT QUANTITY DISCOUNTS WHEN USED TO PROMOTE PRODUCTS OR SERVICES. FOR INFORMATION PLEASE WRITE TO PREMIUM MARKETING DIVISION, THE NEW AMERICAN LIBRARY, INC., 1633 BROADWAY, NEW YORK, NEW YORK 10019.

The first chapter of this book previously appeared in *The Comstock Killers,* the twenty-third volume in this series.

SIGNET TRADEMARK REG. U.S. PAT. OFF. AND FOREIGN COUNTRIES
REGISTERED TRADEMARK—MARCA REGISTRADA
HECHO EN CHICAGO, U.S.A.

SIGNET, SIGNET CLASSIC, MENTOR, PLUME, MERIDIAN and NAL BOOKS are published by The New American Library, Inc., 1633 Broadway, New York, New York 10019

First Printing, December, 1983

1 2 3 4 5 6 7 8 9

PRINTED IN THE UNITED STATES OF AMERICA

The Trailsman

Beginnings . . . they bend the tree and they mark the man. Skye Fargo was born when he was eighteen. Terror was his midwife, vengeance his first cry. Killing spawned Skye Fargo, ruthless, cold-blooded murder. Out of the acrid smoke of gunpowder still hanging in the air, he rose, cried out a promise never forgotten.

The Trailsman, they began to call him, all across the West: searcher, scout, hunter, the man who could see where others only looked, his skills for hire but not his soul, the man who lived each day to the fullest, yet trailed each tomorrow. Skye Fargo, the Trailsman, the seeker who could take the wildness of a land and the wanting of a woman and make them his own.

*Idaho, 1861, when it was
still part of the Oregon Territory,
just west of the Bitterroot Range . . .*

1

He had only two days.

Two days for an almost three-day ride.

Two days to stop them from hanging Nellie Noonan.

The grim facts stabbed at the big man with the lake-blue eyes and the intense, chiseled face. Two days and it wasn't going well and now these two stupid bastards were trying to give him trouble. He spat to one side. The Ovaro had cracked a shoe on a rock and that's why he was at the blacksmith's in this dust-ridden little town with no name, really hardly more than a way station. He'd left the horse with the blacksmith, gone to get a cup of coffee and the two men had been in the smithy's when he'd returned.

"I told you, the horse isn't for sale," Fargo said again, lifting his voice above the pounding of the smithy.

"We made a fair offer, mister," one man said. "When we make an offer, you take it." He left the rest of the threat hanging in a caricature of a smile.

The big man's lake-blue eyes narrowed at the two men. They were cheap drifters, mean-mouthed, gimlet-eyed. He had no time for trouble, no time to risk their getting lucky, no time to haggle with them. He raised his voice again as the blacksmith continued to pound a shoe on his anvil. "Get out of here or you're both dead men," he said.

"You threatening us?" the other said with a sneer.

"I'm promising," Skye Fargo bit out. He watched the two men exchange arrogant glances as the smithy's anvil continued to resound with ear-splitting blows. His hand was poised to whip the big Colt .45 from its holster when the blow came from behind. He felt the sharp explosion of pain as the butt end of a six-gun smashed into the back of his head, felt his legs turn to water and the curtain of blackness sweep over him. He was unconscious as he hit the dirt floor of the blacksmith shop.

Sensations, wet, cold, a stab of pain, they flicked finally inside him, told him he was alive. He forced his eyes open as another splash of cold water hit his face. He blinked, focused and the figure before him took shape, became the blacksmith. The man's angular face peered down at him with concern and Fargo pushed himself up on one elbow, winced at the pain in the back of his head. The blacksmith pushed a wet towel at him. "Here, press this on your head," the man said.

Fargo took the towel, reached one big hand up and back and held the wet cloth to the throbbing spot on his head. His eyes swept the shop with instant apprehension and the smithy answered his gaze.

"They took the Ovaro," he said.

"Sons of bitches," Fargo muttered as he pushed himself to his feet. His mind raced as he put together what had happened. "How many were there?" he asked.

10

"Three," the blacksmith said.

Fargo's eyes bored into the man. "They had you pound that anvil so's I wouldn't hear the one sneaking up behind me," he said.

The smithy nodded, his eyes filled with apology. "I couldn't help it. They told me they'd blow my head off if I didn't stay at the anvil," he said. "They must've seen you come in with your horse because they showed up right after you went for coffee."

Fargo's oath stayed inside him as he saw more precious hours slipping away. "I want a horse," he said to the smithy. The man nodded. "I won't have time to bring him back," Fargo added.

"I'll give you the old bay," the man said. "He'll find his way back." Fargo's hand went to the holster and he swore again as he touched only emptiness. The blacksmith nodded. "The one that bushwhacked you took it, short little weasel with a tan vest. I've only my own gun. I can't give you that."

"Just get the horse," Fargo bit out. He walked to the doorway of the shop, his eyes following the hoofprints in the ground. They led northwest. At least it was in the right direction, he grunted bitterly. The smithy appeared with the old bay, a sturdy horse with legs still good, Fargo saw in one practiced glance.

"The Ovaro's got a good new shoe on," the smithy said, and Fargo started to reach into his pocket. "No," the man said. "This one's on me. Those bastards made me part of their horse-stealin'. I hope you get them."

"Much obliged," Fargo said. "I'll get them." He swung onto the bay, took the horse onto the dusty roadway outside the shop and set off after the hoofprints that stayed nice and clear in soft dirt. His

11

eyes flicked to the sky. Another hour or so of daylight left. Enough, he grunted silently. The three men rode at an easy canter, pulling the Ovaro behind them. They felt secure, stayed on the road a good while before finally turning off into hill country. The old bay moved well enough, Fargo noted, but, bending low in the saddle, he heard the slight rasp deep in the horse's chest and forced himself not to push the animal. He was gaining, anyway, their prints fresher as they slowed going up into the hills. Fargo rode steadily after the trio as he cursed each minute that ticked away. Nellie Noonan's life ebbed away with every goddamn minute. When he reached a hill-country plain, he pushed the old bay harder as the night began to lower. The bastards weren't far ahead, he knew, and he was closing fast when the darkness wrapped itself around the land.

He halted, listened, heard the sounds of horses moving through thick brush and spurred the bay forward slowly, following his ears. He halted as he heard the sounds stop, caught the distant sound of one of the horses blowing air. He dismounted, moved forward on foot, leading the bay behind him. He heard a man's cough, harsh, heavy, the cough of a man with bad lungs. Fargo tethered the bay at the end of a low branch and went forward on steps silent as any mountain cat. The man coughed again, the sound close now. Fargo moved through the trees, came in sight of the three figures, one starting a small campfire, the other two nearby.

Fargo backed away, retraced steps, almost to where he'd left the old bay. He pulled a straight, fresh branch down, broke it off, hefted it in one hand and then drew the double-edged throwing knife from the sheath around his calf. He quickly began to whittle until he had one end of the branch fashioned into a long point. He stood up, tested the branch again— only now it was a crude but effective lance that he weighed in his hand, balanced, let fly for a half-dozen feet. Retrieving the branch, he crept forward again, moved silently through the trees to where they had gotten the small fire started. One man sat in front of the fire with a forked branch, heating strips of beef. Fargo's eyes went to the other two. The one with the tan vest held the big Colt .45 in his hands, examining the gun.

"Jesus, this is a nice piece," Fargo heard him say.

The other one coughed his answer. "We sell it, split the money," he managed between burst of coughing. Fargo moved sideways through the trees, a small circle as, eyes narrowed, he measured space, distance, counted off seconds. The three rotten bastards had already jeopardized Nellie Noonan's life by hours. There was time only to strike swiftly, viciously, each move calculated with deadly accuracy. He circled a half-dozen feet to his left again. He was directly in back of the one at the fire. The short one still admiring the big Colt sat not more than six feet away and the cougher leaned against a tree a few yards on, confidently relaxed.

Fargo's glance swept the scene once more, a final measurement. He rose, the lance he had fashioned in his left hand, the double-edged throwing knife in his right. He flung the knife first, sending the blade hurtling through the night. "Don't see why I can't keep this piece," the one with the tan vest said as he held the Colt. His answer came wrapped in cold steel that hurtled into the left side of his neck and came partly out the right side. Fargo didn't wait to see him drop the Colt, grab at his neck with both

13

hands as a torrent of red cascaded from his mouth. The Trailsman was already running, powerful leg muscles driving him across the ground. He slammed into the figure at the fire with the force of a stampeding buffalo and the man catapulted forward into the fire, his face smashing into the flaming pieces of wood. His scream split the night but Fargo was leaping, diving over the fire, executing a somersault to land on his back on the other side. He was rolling into the brush as the third man got his first shot off, followed by two more wild shots.

Fargo, in the brush, glimpsed the other man rolling on the ground, screaming in anguish as little pieces of flame danced over his face. Fargo rolled again, deeper into the brush, heard two more shots explode. They were closer, whistling over his head and he ducked around the trunk of a hackberry. He shifted the makeshift lance to his right hand, crouched as the third man came toward him, gun in his hand, peering into the darkness. Fargo's arm was drawn back when he straightened, hurled the crude lance at his target and dropped to the ground at once. The man spun, fired at the sound. The lance struck him alongside the temple as he twisted away, yet with enough force to send him sprawling backward. As the man landed on his back Fargo darted forward, scooped up the length of branch and drove forward with it. The man started to bring his gun up as Fargo drove the lance into his solar plexus, all his strength and weight behind it. The crude point made a jagged tear of a hole as it plunged into the man, rupturing innards, tearing aside tissue. The man emitted a deep gargling sound as his torso jerked convulsively. Fargo stepped back, left the crude lance

14

shaking violently in place as the man's body jerked in its convulsive death throes.

He turned away, took two steps and emerged from the brush to retrieve his gun. It lay beside the still figure that continued to spill red from its gaping mouth. He bent over, yanked his throwing knife free, cleaned the blade on the grass and put it away. He was swinging onto the Ovaro when he cast a glance at the third figure lying to one side, long, low moans emanating from what had once been a face but seemed now to be only a charred, still-smoking side of meat. Fargo wheeled the Ovaro in a tight circle and headed from the scene, anxious only to make up time. They had taken almost three hours from him, and from Nellie Noonan, and he cursed their rotten hearts as he rode on. The night was deep when he finally halted. A tired horse could still make time, an exhausted one was certain trouble. He unsaddled the Ovaro and stretched himself out on a soft bed of elf's-cap moss, let his tired body ease itself into relaxed calm. Once again, he went over the beginning of it, the little town of Flatwheel and the saloon in the center of main street.

He'd stopped in at the saloon to see Charley Oxman. Charley had been bartending there for almost two years, since he had his leg broken in three places by a steer. His steer-wrestling days over, he'd turned to tending bar and they had talked about old days and old ways. Fargo remembered how he had a shot glass of bourbon almost to his lips when he heard the man's voice carry through the hum of conversation. He'd frozen in place, fingers curling tight around the shot glass.

"First woman they ever hung in Brushville," the man's voice had said. "Nellie Noonan's her name."

Fargo had almost shattered the shot glass in his hand, lowered it to the bar and turned, his eyes boring into the man, a thin-faced, slight-built, balding man wearing a waistcoat and fancy suspenders, talking to a bearded companion. "Say that again, mister," Fargo growled. "About Nellie Noonan."

The slight-built man turned, leveled a glance of mild curiosity at him. "I said they're going to hang her," he repeated.

Fargo had snapped out steel-muscled arms, seized the man by the shirtfront and lifted him from the ground as though he were a child. "You talking big, telling stories, mister?" he rasped. "You lying, spreading rumors?"

The man's eyes filled with fear and awe as his feet dangled in the air. "No, Jesus, no stories," he said. "I just left Brushville a few days back. I wouldn't make up somethin' like that."

Fargo forced his hands to unclasp and he lowered the man to the ground, saw him swallow hard and relief come into his fear-filled eyes. "Jesus, mister, you got an interest or somethin'?" the man muttered.

"Nellie Noonan," Fargo growled. "Nellie's no candidate for hanging. Never could be, not Nellie. Something's wrong, some kind of mistake. Tell me more."

The man shrugged. "They say she shot and killed Judge Counsil," he said.

"Nellie Noonan? Never, not her. There's something wrong," Fargo snapped back.

"They say she still had the gun in her hand when they reached the judge," the man answered. "Judge Counsil was a powerful man in Brushville, nobody you go around shooting."

16

"It's a lie, a goddamn lie," Fargo flung back. "I know Nellie Noonan. She wouldn't shoot a soul."

The man shrugged again. "Heard she'd been having an affair with the judge and tried to push him for more money. He said no, walked out on her and she up and shot him."

"Never," Fargo roared. "That's either some big damn mistake or it's a pack of goddamn lies."

The man swallowed hard again. "Don't get mad at me, mister. All I know is what I heard. They're going to hang her Thursday," he said.

"Thursday?" Fargo remembered exploding. "Damn, that's only two days from now." He'd spun on his heel and raced out of the saloon, leaving a torrent of oaths behind him. Two days. Not enough time, he'd swore as he vaulted onto the Ovaro. Not enough time, but he had to somehow make it enough. He'd raced from the town, crossed the Salmon River and galloped north and west. He'd made good time until the horse cracked the hoof and he wound up in the smithy's. The rest needed no reliving, three hours spent, three hours that belonged to Nellie Noonan. He cursed softly, put his arms behind his head and old memories swam into his mind. Nellie Noonan had always been one of the good people in this world, pretty and sweet and quick with a smile. But it was so much more than that. Nellie was one of the caring people, one of those few who put the needs of others before their own needs.

Nellie Noonan a killer? Fargo gave a harsh, wry snort. Never, not her. He hadn't seen her in three years but that made no difference. He knew Nellie well, knew what she could do, but more important, what she couldn't do. Something was wrong. Something stunk like a carp in the sun for three days, he thought. He closed his eyes, forced sleep on himself and was in the saddle again at dawn. He crossed to the edge of the Bitterroot Range where a good trail let him make time, the ground kept smoothed by the trappers and their pack mules and the fur traders who drove their wagons as far north as Payette Lake.

Brushville lay just west of the Bitterroot and he held to a steady pace, reined up only when he caught sight of the five near-naked horsemen on a distant ridge. He squinted in the morning sun but they were too far away to pick out markings. The Northern Shoshones rode this land, as did the Nez Percé, and the Kiowa came over the Montana border all too often. He hung back until they disappeared down the other side of the ridge, anxious only to avoid further delays. When they were out of sight he spurred his horse forward, continued on with a steady pace. Three hours were proving damned hard to make up and he pushed the pinto until night fell once more and he bedded down, gave the horse and himself as much rest as he dared. He was in the saddle again as dawn painted its pink edges along the mountain tops.

It was Thursday, dammit, he thought through tightened lips, and he'd still a good way to go to reach Brushville. He bent low in the saddle, cutting down wind resistance as the Ovaro's gleaming black fore- and hindquarters and pure white midsection glistened in the sun. He watched the golden sphere climb into the noon sky and the dryness in his mouth grew bitter. He flung an oath into the hot, dry wind and listened to the steady drumbeat of the pinto's hooves. Fields of lavender-blue chickory blossomed on his left and on the right, bright pink rockrose made the high banks shimmer with beauty. Damn, it was a day for life and beauty, he thought, not a day for a hanging. And surely not Nellie Noonan's hanging. He'd stopped watching the sun move across the afternoon sky when Brushville came into sight, nestled at the foothills of the Bitterroot Range, a town that had set itself at the start of the north passage into Washington state and became the jumping off place for every wagon train and sodbuster headed to the Far West.

Brushville had sprouted with the traffic, had stores and a proper bank where settlers could get cash for supplies and a fancy house separate from the saloon. Nellie had opened a piece-goods store when he last saw her and was happy and well. The flash of remembering brought a grimness to his mouth and he spurred the pinto full out for the last few hundred yards, slowing only when he reached town.

The wide main street had the usual collection of wagons and horses tied to hitching posts. Fargo's eyes swept down the dirt street, across the figures moving back and forth. No crowd gathering, he noticed, no loungers waiting alongside the wooden buildings. He wanted to seize hope but could feel only a grim apprehension. He reined up outside a window with gold letters painted onto the glass.

SHERIFF'S OFFICE—R. COLEMAN, he read as he swung down from the pinto and walked through the open door. A man looked up from a battered desk in the front room—beefy-faced, with gray, wary eyes, a frame too thick around the middle but with shoulders still bearlike.

"You the sheriff?" Fargo bit out and the tension was in his voice and in the ice blue of his eyes.

"That's right." The man nodded. "Rob Coleman."

"Heard you had a hanging set for today," Fargo said.

The man nodded again. "You come to watch?"

"I came to stop it," Fargo snapped back. He saw the gray, wary eyes grow more wary, narrow a fraction as the man took in his big, powerfully muscled frame, the intenseness of his chiseled features.

"Either way, you're too late," Sheriff Coleman said. "We did it yesterday, change in plans."

Fargo's words came from his lips with ominous slowness. "You hung Nellie Noonan yesterday," he repeated.

Sheriff Coleman felt a stab of uncomfortableness as the big man's eyes speared into him as though he were a fly on a pin. "That's right," he said. "Sorry."

"Not near as sorry as you're going to be," Fargo said, and his words were sheathed in ice.

2

Sheriff Coleman let the big man's words hang in the air. No empty threats, no hollow bragging in them, he realized, and felt both discomfort and alarm as he took in the figure before him. This was a man who could make one hell of a lot of trouble, the sheriff thought to himself, and pushed away the stab of nervousness in the pit of his stomach. "What's your name, mister?" he asked.

"Fargo. Skye Fargo," the big man said. "Some call me the Trailsman."

The sheriff licked his lips that had gone dry. "Heard of you," he said unhappily. "You kin to her?"

"She was a special person. Nellie Noonan couldn't kill anyone. Something stinks like hell here," Fargo said.

Sheriff Coleman summoned up bluster. "Now, you hold on, Fargo. You just got here. You've no right saying a thing like that." He frowned.

"Hell, I don't," Fargo roared back. "I heard the story about her killing this Judge Counsil and it's a goddamn lie."

"How the hell do you know that?" the sheriff threw

back. "You weren't around. You didn't even know Judge Counsil."

"I knew Nellie Noonan. That's enough for me."

He saw the sheriff's eyes grow smaller, shrewder. "Maybe you didn't know her as well as you thought you did," the man returned.

"No, *you* didn't know her well enough. That's where somebody made a mistake," Fargo said with grim bitterness. He leaned forward, palms flattened on the sheriff's desk. "It was a mistake or it was murder. Either way, somebody's going to pay. You can damn well be sure of that." He saw the sheriff swallow. He straightened, his eyes blue hard. "Why'd you do it yesterday? Why the hurry to hang her? Who was nervous?"

"Nobody," the sheriff answered, but Fargo caught the thinness in his voice. "Judge Counsil was a very popular man. It was decided there might be a lynch mob if we waited."

"Who decided?" Fargo spat out derisively.

"The town board. The mayor and the others. I just take orders," Sheriff Coleman said.

"You take the wrong orders, you pay too," Fargo said, and he turned, strode to the door, paused to look back at the sheriff. "Where's Nellie now?"

"You've got to be kin to claim her body."

"Where is she?" Fargo growled, spearing the man again with blue-ice eyes.

"Joe Holder, end of the street. He's our undertaker."

Fargo walked from the sheriff's office, headed down the street, staying close to the buildings. With a quick hop, he ducked between two frame structures, pressed himself against one and peered out into the street. It didn't take Sheriff Coleman more than a half minute

22

to hurry from his office and rush up the street. Fargo watched him go, waited until he went into a brick-and-wood building with the sign BRUSHVILLE BANK outside the front door. Fargo's grunt was a short, bitter sound as he stepped from the building and continued down the street. The gray purple of dusk had begun to settle itself over Brushville, and beyond, the tall peaks of the Bitterroot Range filled the last of the day sky. He halted at the last building in the town proper; a single word was crudely painted on the side of the narrow structure: UNDERTAKER.

Fargo entered the door to see a thin man with a sour face and eyes that blinked with constant nervousness. The man looked up from behind a plain wood table. Fargo's glance took in the closed door to a room behind the small front office. The man's blinking eyes framed the question as his sour face studied the newcomer. "Came to see Nellie Noonan," Fargo said. "You the undertaker?"

The man's eyes blinked faster as he nodded. "Can't let you see her," he said. "Box is sealed. We don't open boxes when they're sealed." Fargo's stare pierced the undertaker and Joe Holder looked away quickly, fiddled with a drawer in the table.

"Who told you to seal it?" Fargo said.

"Town board," the man said.

"Goddamn convenient," Fargo muttered as thoughts tumbled inside his head. The stink was growing stronger. There was no way to make sense of it yet, but something was very wrong. More than just the hanging, he was convinced now. He knew that was wrong for his own reasons. But there was more. He'd damn well find out and sombody would pay. The undertaker's words cut into his thoughts.

"You want to see her personal things?" the man

asked. "Got 'em here." He pulled out the little drawer on the other side of the table, brought out a small leather sack and spilled the contents on the table. Fargo stared down at a gold locket on a gold chain, two silver bracelets, a small red purse. "Only a few pieces of silver and a missal inside it," Joe Holder said, gesturing toward the purse.

Fargo continued to stare at the gold locket and the silver bracelets, his lips pursed. His eyes were narrowed as he lifted them to the undertaker. "I want to see her, one last time."

"Forget it. I told you, we don't open up sealed boxes," Joe Holder said. "We bury her tomorrow when Seth gets back. He's our gravedigger."

Fargo gathered the jewelry and purse, put everything back in the little sack. "I'll take these," he said, shoving the sack into a back pocket.

The undertaker pulled a little pad from the drawer. "Sign or make your mark for them," he said, watched as the big man wrote his name. Joe Holder's frown gathered and Fargo saw a new note of respect come into the man's eyes.

"Skye Fargo," Joe Holder read aloud. "The one they call the Trailsman?" he asked. Fargo nodded at the man. "She never said anything about you being a friend of hers," the undertaker muttered.

"Guess there was no reason to," Fargo said. "Now you know." He turned from the man and strode into the dusk, hurried across the street and this time ducked behind a watering trough. He watched as Joe Holder emerged from the narrow building, pausing only to lock the door before rushing up the street. Fargo followed in the last dim light, keeping his distance until the man went into the bank. He stepped between two buildings again and waited until Sheriff Coleman and the undertaker emerged, faces lined with concern as they talked excitedly to each other. Fargo faded into the darkness as the two men went past, waited a few moments longer and then moved into the open again. He strolled toward the saloon only a dozen yards away, pushed the swinging doors open and entered.

The night had just begun and there were only a few customers in the place. He saw the bartender, a round-shouldered man with shrewd, watery-blue eyes, watch him enter and move toward the bar. "What's your pleasure, stranger?" the man called out.

"Bourbon," Fargo said as he leaned elbows on the bar, let his eyes move around the saloon. Two men sat at a table with a bottle of rotgut between them. Another pair of bearded oldsters hung at the far end of the bar. Three lone drinkers were scattered around the rest of the room and an elderly black man prepared to play an old, nicked upright piano by adjusting the stool and polishing the keys. The bartender put the shot glass of bourbon before him and Fargo lifted it, took a deep draw of it. "Heard you had a first here yesterday," he said as he savored the strong, warming flavor of good bourbon.

"You mean hanging a woman?" the bartender said. "Yep, that was a first, all right."

"You saw it, I expect?" Fargo asked casually.

"Wasn't much to see," the bartender answered. "They had a pillowcase over her head."

"A pillowcase over her head?" Fargo echoed. "Why?"

"The town board felt it was only proper that way, her being a woman."

"Mighty considerate of them. Hope she appreciated it." Fargo was unable to keep the edge from his voice. "Who are the proper-minded gents on this town board?" he asked, drawing on his drink again.

"Tim Smith, the mayor, Charley Evans, president of the bank, Judge Counsil before she killed him and Sheriff Coleman," the bartender said, and Fargo saw the man's eyes narrow a fraction. "You ask a lot of questions, stranger."

"All for Nellie Noonan." Fargo finished his bourbon and watched the surprise flood the bartender's face. He turned and walked from the saloon, the man's stare following him. Outside in the night, he slowly strolled down the street as more men began to enter the saloon, picked up the Ovaro where he'd left him and crossed to a narrow space between buildings, moved through to emerge at the rear of the line of houses.

He made his way slowly down behind the buildings until he reached the narrow structure that was the undertaker's parlor. A small clearing set back from the rear of the building and beyond it, woodland. He tied the Ovaro inside the tree line and returned to the narrow structure. A butcher wagon that had been converted to a hearse rested at one side of the little clearing, painted black with the drop-leaf back door hung with a black, fringed curtain. Double doors came together at the rear of the building, latched at the center. Fargo reached down and drew the thin, double-edged throwing knife he carried in a calf holster. Working carefully, he slid the blade through the slit between the two doors, sliding it back and forth. He felt the latch move. It wasn't much of a latch, he realized gratefully as he continued to press the thin blade through the slit between the doors. He slid the blade upward through the tiny space between the latch and the wood until he felt the tip of the blade catch into the space. He paused, carefully flattened the hilt of the blade against the doors and pressed upward again. His lips drew back in satisfaction as he felt the latch slide open and he pulled one of the two doors toward him, just wide enough to slip into the building.

He halted inside, frowned. The blackness wasn't as total as he expected. A faint, flickering light drifted into the room through an open doorway and allowed him to discern the outline of pine caskets piled atop each other. The flickering light beckoned from the adjoining room and he moved toward it, his footsteps silent as a cougar on the prowl. Reaching the open doorway, he peered into the other room and saw more pine boxes. His hand went to the butt of the Colt .45 in its holster as he moved forward. He saw the candle first, not much more than a stub, placed on the floor, sending out flickering light to illuminate the long, pine box and the figure kneeling in front of it, back to him. The figure wore a buckskin jacket and a wide-brimmed hat pushed back. Fargo heard the sound of nails being lifted as the figure pried at one end of the pine box with a screwdriver. He took another step forward.

"Don't move," he said. "Turn around nice and slow."

He saw the figure stiffen, draw the screwdriver back from one end of the box, begin to turn toward him. He felt his brows lift at the face that turned toward him, round, brown eyes, a little stubby nose, slighty plump cheeks, prettiness framed by brown hair pulled up tight. He stared at the girl for a moment as he dropped his hand from the Colt.

"Who the hell are you?" he slid at her.

Her answer came with the flick of her wrist as she

flung the screwdriver, a short, sharp upward flip. She was too near for him to avoid the blow completely and he felt the stab of pain as the screwdriver hit him high on the forehead as he twisted away. He swore, saw her leap to her feet and start to dart around the pine box. He spurted after her and she changed directions, quick as a gazelle in the flickering light, and headed for the twin doors at the rear of the building. She darted between two empty caskets and he raced past both, dived as she tried to dart by him, his long arms winding around her legs.

"Damn," he heard her swear as she hit the floor. She tried to get a leg free and kick at him, but he kept a tight hold of her, worked his grip upward, felt smooth, firm skin, slender thighs. "You bastard," he heard her hiss as she struggled, tried to pull her legs free. But he kept his hold, swung with his shoulders and flipped her onto her back. He let go of her legs and dived upward in one motion, pinned her arms to the floor with his hands and used his body to keep her from trying to knee him in the groin.

"Cut it out, dammit," he growled.

"Damn you," she hissed, lifted her head, brought it around and started to sink her teeth into his arm. He pulled back, let go of one wrist. Her hand came up instantly, fingernails clawing at his face, but he blocked the blow, slammed her wrist down onto the floor again. Her legs tried to lift, kick at him but he held them down with his body.

"Will you simmer down, dammit?" he rasped.

"Bastard," she hissed, tried again to wriggle free. She attempted to bring her head around again when he heard the sound of hoofbeats coming to a halt just outside the front of the building. She heard them too, ceased struggling to freeze in silence. Fargo, his head raised, heard the voices as the horsemen dismounted, caught the sound of the door being opened. Sheriff Coleman's voice echoed through the rooms.

"Two men inside and two outside," the sheriff barked. "From dark to dawn until this is done with."

Another voice, alarm in it, interrupted. "What's that light?" it asked.

"Get your asses in there and find out," the sheriff ordered.

Fargo heard the hurried pounding of boots, sprang from the girl to land on the tips of his toes in a crouch, the big Colt in his hand. "Let's get out of here," he said, and saw the girl, sitting up, her eyes peering at him as a frown dug into her brow. Fargo saw two men barrel into the room, their eyes focusing on the candle on the floor. Fargo pressed the trigger of the big Colt and the candle blew apart in a shower of hot wax and spirals of tiny flame.

"Jesus," he heard one of the men mutter as the room plunged into darkness. The sheriff's voice came from the outside office.

"Get a lamp lighted, dammit," the man shouted. One of the two men in the room fired two shots and Fargo lowered his crouch, hit the floor as two more shots peppered the wall behind him. Wild shots, yet dangerous. He looked around for the girl and held the oath inside himself. She was gone, vanished and he got to his feet, sprinted for the twin doors at the rear of the building. He holstered the Colt as he lowered one shoulder, slammed into the doors to send both flying open. Outside, he saw the figure racing from around the corner of the house to cut him off. He yanked the Colt out again as the man turned in on him, ducked low as the other men hurtled at him. He brought the Colt up in a back-hand arc, smashed the gun barrel into the side of the man's face and the figure toppled sideways, went down on one knee, then the ground.

Fargo continued racing forward, reached the trees where the Ovaro was hitched and ducked low as a shot whistled through the darkness. He heard Sheriff Coleman shouting as he came around the side of the building but Fargo vaulted onto the pinto's back and sent the horse plunging into the woods. He galloped a few dozen yards and reined up, leaned to one side in the saddle, ears straining. He straightened up after a moment. They weren't following. They were more concerned with checking out the undertaker's parlor and making it secure than giving chase. Fargo drew a deep breath, waited quietly in the saddle as the questions whirled inside him. Who was the girl? What was she doing there? Why was she trying to pry open Nellie Noonan's casket? Or was it someone else's box? No matter, she could probably give him some answers he needed. He wouldn't attempt slipping inside the funeral parlor now. They'd be alert and on guard. He'd try to pick up her tracks. She'd disappeared like a wraith in the night but she was no wraith, not that pretty, plump-cheeked spitfire. She'd leave tracks and, his lips a thin line, he sat the Ovaro and let almost an hour go by before moving the horse slowly back toward the end of town. Right now, he knew only one thing. The smell of it kept growing worse. He wanted to cling to the thin edge of hope but he didn't dare. There was too much chance for bitter answers, yet.

He came into sight of the narrow structure, swung from the Ovaro and moved forward on foot. The rear doors had been closed and latched again, he

30

saw. The sheriff had posted the two outside guards at the front of the building, the other two covering the rear from inside. Fargo crept forward, almost to the two latched doors. A waxing half-moon afforded enough light for him to make out marks on the sandy, loose soil. He saw where he'd raced out of the building, met the other man coming in from the side. The dirt lay scattered where they had met and where the others had come up. He bent low, went over the tracks again. There were no others. He moved forward, this time to the very edge of the building, sent his gaze sliding along the side of the structure and heard the tiny sound inside himself as he spied her tracks. She had turned the minute she was outside and ran tight along the side of the building.

He followed, the footprints clear now, since she had run with heels digging hard into the ground. She had crossed a small clear space at the side of the building and he probed into a thicket of mulberry bushes and halted. The footprints changed into hoofprints. She'd had a horse waiting and his eyes lifted, saw where she had charged on through the mulberry bushes, a path of broken edges and crushed berries. He turned, trotted back to retrieve the Ovaro and followed through the mulberries to where she'd swung out onto the road from Brushville, riding hard. She had stayed on the road for almost a half mile and suddenly veered from it in a sharp right turn to cut across a field filled with wild bergamot, leaving a clear, trampled path in the flowers.

A house came into sight on a slight rise in the field, dark except for a lone light from one window. He slowed, made a half circle around the house to approach from the side and saw, in surprise, that it was but half a house, the rear section still only framework. Fargo moved closer, dismounted and approached the finished half of the house. A lone lamp sent a long, thin path of yellow from the window and he crept to one side of the window frame, peered into what turned out to be a sparsely furnished bedroom, a brass bed to one side, a battered, white dresser and a torn stuffed chair the only pieces in the room. The girl, her back to him, was turning down the sheet on the bed. She wore a short, light blue nightdress that came only midway down her thigh to reveal tanned, firm young legs with long, beautifully shaped calves. She turned toward the lamp and he saw that the brown hair was no longer pulled atop her head but fell loosely around her face, giving a softer line to her plump-cheeked countenance. He watched as she crawled under the sheet, reached out to turn off the lamp and he spotted the long-barreled Spencer standing against the bed, the comb of the rifle just at eye level with her as she lay in the brass bed. She could reach out and have it in hand in a split second, he saw with narrowed eyes as she turned the lamp out and blackness filled the room at once.

His lips pursed as he let his options revolve in his mind. Trying to get into the house and take her by surprise was a high-risk operation; the rifle was too close to her. From the way she'd fought him at the undertaker's, a knock on the door could also bring a blast of lead. He decided against either course and moved from the window, retreated to where he'd left the Ovaro. He'd wait for morning, he decided, let surprise be all his way. He led the Ovaro into a thicket of dwarf maple and put his blanket down. He lay down and let the questions tumble in his mind, new ones springing up at almost every turn. Why had they hung Nellie Noonan? That still stayed as number one. Or, and his lips became a grim line, why did they claim they had? One more piece had added itself to the questions, though it explained nothing. Steps had been taken to see that Nellie's casket remained untouched. The sheriff had descended with sentries to put in place. Plainly that had been the result of the hurried conference at the bank. They had sealed the pine box and now they'd placed guards around it. Why? What were they so damned concerned about? Fargo's lips stayed a tight line as he took out the little leather pouch the undertaker had given him. He opened it, stared down at the gold chain and locket, the silver bracelets.

He grunted as he put the jewelry away again. He was growing more certain with every passing minute that he had one answer. But being certain and knowing were two different things and he had to know, to be sure, to see with his own eyes. And now the girl had come along to add more questions. He turned on his side, the big Colt beside his hand, closed his eyes in sleep. He wanted to be ready for morning and a brown-haired spitfire. He slept as he had learned to sleep, as the cougar sleeps, the inner senses always alert, always awake. But the night passed quietly and the dawn light slipped over the land as he rose. The house seemed stranger in the light, the rear half more glaringly unfinished. It was still quiet as he used his canteen to wash and stayed in the trees to wait. He was resting on one knee when he saw the window pushed open. The door swung out a few minutes later and he stepped to the edge of the maples. She came out, still wearing the short light blue nightdress, headed for a well on the lovely, tanned legs, moving with a graceful, sliding motion that let the nightdress fall rhythmically against a nice, round rear. She carried a large, heavy white pitcher, set it down as she pulled the bucket up from the well. He let her fill the pitcher before he stepped from the trees.

"Remember me?" he said softly, and the girl spun, modest breasts pushing hard against the nightdress for an instant. The surprise that flooded her plump-cheeked face gave way quickly to a wary frown. "You didn't wait for me," Fargo said, letting himself sound hurt.

Her eyes narrowed further. "How'd you find me?" she muttered crossly.

"Got lucky," he said, and moved a few steps closer to her.

She made a disbelieving, derisive sound. "Who are you?" she asked.

"I'm asking, you're answering, honey," Fargo told her, and watched her study him for a moment. She used a little half shrug to cover the movement of her arm as she flung the pitcher of water. It hit him full in the face and he blinked in automatic reaction, pulled his dripping eyelids open to see her streaking for the open doorway of the house. "*Goddamn,*" he swore as he raced after her, brought her down with a flying tackle just as she reached the door. She landed in the house and he got to one knee, yanked her by the full, brown hair and spun her around.

"Owoo!" she screamed.

"No redo of last night, dammit," Fargo rasped, brought her head down sharply against the floor.

"Ow! You're hurting me," she gasped.

"I haven't started," he said. "Now you're going to answer my questions. You can do it the easy way or the hard way. I don't much care which, but you're

34

going to answer. You've got three seconds to make up your mind."

He kept his grip on her hair, pulling it tight, and her eyes peered into his, thoughts racing through her head as she tried to read behind his lake-blue eyes. "Let go of my hair," she muttered.

"You going to behave? I saw that old Spencer in the other room," he said.

She took another moment, finally nodded, winced as the motion pulled her hair in his big hand. He opened his fingers, drew his hand back and rose to his feet, yanked her up with him. His quick glance took in the room, a worn couch at one side, a few old chairs, a peg-leg table near the couch. His glance returned to the girl, saw her studying him. "You wanted to get out of there last night, too. You're not one of them," she said.

"Them?" he questioned.

"Sheriff Coleman's crew," she said.

"You were trying to open Nellie Noonan's casket. Why?" Fargo pushed at her crisply.

He saw her eyes grow shrewd. "Curious."

His voice took on a hard edge. "You can do better than that."

She met the sharpness that had come into the lake-blue eyes, drew a deep breath. "Let's go into the kitchen. I put coffee on," she said, waited for his permission. He nodded and she turned, went into the next room and he followed, unable to not enjoy the way the short nightdress fell against her round little rear and the nice turn of her firm, tanned legs. Coffee perked in an old, green, enameled pot on a small stove. She took two tin mugs from a shelf, poured both full of the steaming brew and lowered herself into a chair by a small table. She crossed her legs and he saw very pretty, dimpled knees. He sipped the coffee, stayed on his feet.

"Let's start over," he said.

Her eyes grew stubborn at once. "Answering goes both ways," she said.

"Fair enough," he agreed. "You've a name. Start with that."

"Bonnie," she said. "Bonnie Akins. And you?"

"Skye Fargo. Some call me the Trailsman."

She gave a little sound. "The Trailsman. That's why you found me."

"Now, why were you trying to open Nellie Noonan's casket?" Fargo questioned, his voice suddenly harsh.

"To see if she was really inside," Bonnie Akins answered. "What'd you want there?" she threw back.

"Seems we both had the same reason." Fargo saw her lips part in surprise. "What if I were to tell you it's not Nellie in that casket?"

Her brown eyes were round saucers as she answered. "It was sealed. How would you know that?"

"I don't know, but I'm getting pretty damn sure," Fargo said grimly, taking a long sip of the coffee.

"Why does it matter to you?" Bonnie asked.

"Nellie Noonan was an old friend, a special person," Fargo said. "When I heard they were going to hang her, I hightailed it here to stop them. But they'd pushed it up a day. Something stinks here. Nellie didn't kill that damn Judge Counsil and she's not in that box."

Fargo watched Bonnie's eyes stay on him, a mixture of emotions he couldn't sort out racing through their brown depths. Her lips moved before the words came out and he saw her tongue flick out to wipe the dryness from them. "What makes you so damn sure?" she asked, almost hesitantly.

He took the little sack from his pocket and spilled the contents on the table. "Holder gave me these. She was wearing them, he said. Her personal possessions," Fargo answered, and the hardness was in his voice again. Bonnie Akins frowned up at him. "Nellie Noonan couldn't wear jewelry, especially gold or silver. It made her skin break out in a rash. She never wore the stuff, never."

He felt the frown dig into his brow as Bonnie suddenly buried her face in her hands. "My God, oh, my God," he heard her murmur, words muffled in sobs. He watched her shudder, reached out and closed one big hand over her shoulder. The trembling was real, coursing through her body. He kept his hands on her shoulder, a firm pressure, until the trembling halted.

"You've more to say. Out with it," he ordered, not ready to give sympathy yet. "Why were you trying to look into that box?"

She took her hands from her face and he saw the real pain in her round, brown eyes. "To see if it was my sister in there," she flung at him.

Fargo felt the surprise catch at his breath. "Your sister?" he echoed.

She nodded, bit her lower lip with her teeth. "It has to be," she murmured despairingly. "It has to be."

"You recognize that locket and the bracelets as hers?" he questioned.

"No, I didn't know half the jewelry she had," Bonnie said.

"Then why do you think it's your sister in that box?" Fargo asked.

"Because the things you just told me fit in," she said, and the pain in her eyes was too real to fake.

37

"You're not making much sense out of anything," Fargo growled.

She grimaced. "I guess not. I'd best explain about Carrie, first. She's six years older than I am. I lived with an aunt in Owlseville the past four years and came here only a few months ago when she died."

"You saying you and your sister weren't close?" Fargo asked.

"No, we were very close. We wrote regularly and visited often enough. We just didn't live together for the past four years. Carrie was always the wild one and when I came to live here I found out she hadn't changed. And I was still the kid sister. She wouldn't listen to me."

"All this doesn't tell me why you think your sister might be in that box and not Nellie Noonan," Fargo cut in.

"I saw Joe Holder and two men take her with them last week," she said. "I was just coming home when they went off with her. I didn't think much about it. She knew Joe Holder and I didn't even think about it when she didn't come back that night. Carrie stayed out lots, I just wondered some when she didn't come back the next day. But when she didn't come back at all I got worried."

"You go to see Joe Holder?" Fargo asked.

"Yes and he said he hadn't taken Carrie anywhere, the rotten little weasel. He said I must've seen somebody else. Then when all that business about Nellie Noonan broke and they quick hung her so's you couldn't see her face, I began to really worry. Carrie's the same size and build as Nellie Noonan. I know, I've seen them together often enough in Nellie's piece-goods store. Now everything you've said fits in," Bonnie told him.

"It doesn't fit right," Fargo answered, and Bonnie's eyes questioned. "If they wanted to get rid of your sister for some reason, they could've just done it. They didn't need a fancy story about Nellie Noonan and Judge Counsil to do that."

"Meaning what?" Bonnie frowned.

"The tail doesn't wag the dog. It's the other way around. Nellie's at the heart of it, somehow. If they used your sister it was because they needed a stand-in for Nellie," he said. "But why? What the hell does it all mean?"

"Don't know more than you do on that, Fargo," Bonnie Akins said. "I don't understand any of it."

"That makes two of us. But I'm sure as hell going to find out."

"You can include me in," Bonnie said darkly.

"I work alone. You'll get in my way."

Her eyes flashed. "One way or the other. You can count on it." She shrugged. He let her words circle inside him. She was more than stubborn. She had a burning stake in whatever had been done and she wouldn't turn away. She'd be less trouble where he could keep an eye on her, he decided.

"I call the shots or you're out," he growled.

She nodded agreement, finished her coffee and threw out the bitter grounds at the bottom of the cup. She rose, tartness in her voice. "I'd like to get dressed," she said.

"Be my guest." He leaned back in the chair, watched her go into the bedroom with her half-sliding, fluid walk. He sat back in the chair and went over Bonnie's story in his mind. It added more questions than it answered, he mused, still deep in thought when she reappeared wearing a dark set of riding britches and a pale lemon shirt. He let appreciation show in a

39

glance that lingered on the soft twin curves that rose up against the lemon shirt, still modest yet firm and full.

"What now?" Bonnie asked.

"They're burying her today. We'll pay our respects," Fargo said.

"I'll get my horse." She went behind the house to reappear a moment later in the saddle of a brown mare. He swung onto the pinto. "Cemetery's outside town," she said, and led the way as he rode beside her. He saw her pretty, plump-cheeked face drawn in on itself and her lips pressed hard onto each other.

"Say it, whatever it is," he remarked.

"Doesn't seem right, us paying respects and we don't know for sure to whom," she said.

"I'll be paying them, whoever's in that box," Fargo said. "That's all that matters, paying them."

"Yes, I suppose so, seeing it that way," Bonnie agreed, her face still tight. "What happens after?"

"I wait, then do some digging." He saw the distaste fill her quick glance. "No other way," he said gently. "I'm not much for it, either, but I've no choice. I only know one thing so far. They hung somebody. Maybe it was Nellie. That's the first thing I've got to find out for sure." He saw Bonnie nod with her lips pulled tight against each other. "I'll be finding out for both of us," he said, and she blinked at him, a flash of understanding in her eyes as she fought back tears.

He rode slowly, his eyes peering forward, but he felt her watching him. Bonnie Akins studied the big man riding beside her, took in the intense, chiseled handsomeness, the charged power of him. "Nellie Noonan must've been some woman to bring a man like you running," she remarked.

"She was, but not the way you're thinking."

"Want to tell me more?"

"Sometime, maybe," he said as the horses crested a small hillock and the cemetery came into view, cutting off anything further he might have said. Fargo felt surprise at the size of the graveyard and at some of the headstones.

"It doesn't take only from Brushville," Bonnie said. "Folks far away as Ashland and all the small towns around here use it."

He nodded, rode closer and moved toward a thin figure leaning against a long-handled shovel beside an open, freshly dug area. Seth, the gravedigger, Fargo noted to himself and saw the man watch him out of tired, sunken eyes. He halted the pinto, Bonnie moving beside him, sat in silence, waiting, and only the call of a scarlet tanager broke the stillness. Fargo guessed they'd waited perhaps an hour when he saw the small procession moving toward them. Joe Holder's converted, black butcher wagon led the way with two horsemen riding behind it. Fargo recognized Sheriff Coleman coming up behind with three more horsemen and he peered at the two-seat spring wagon at the rear, rigged with a parasol over the seats. He saw three men in the wagon, one a minister, the other two in frock coats.

"Preacher Halsman, the mayor, Tim Smith, and Charley Evans," Bonnie said, picking up his thoughts.

The procession made a slow circle, came to a halt on the opposite side of the freshly dug, open pit. Fargo met the sheriff's harsh glance with bland acknowledgment, let his eyes go to the converted butcher wagon where Joe Holder and two men were pulling the unmarked pine box out. He watched them lower it into the ground with ropes, then step

41

back. His eyes went to the mayor of Brushville and appraised a square-faced man with pepper-and-salt hair, blue-gray eyes in a face that had learned to hide a lot behind a thin air of authority. His glance flicked to the banker. Charley Evans met his eyes with a combination of curiosity and imperiousness, the man's very stance one of a bantam rooster, puffed up and strutting, his face showing signs of too much easy living in little red veins that made his cheeks a network of erratic lines. The preacher, younger than the other two men, seemed nervous, his narrow face distinctly uncomfortable. He stepped from the spring wagon first and the other two men followed. He moved to the edge of the grave, his face taking on a mixture of compassion and severity.

"We commit thee, Nellie Noonan, into the hands of the Lord," he began. "We pass no further mortal judgment on your crimes."

Fargo's voice cut through the still air as an ax cuts through buttermilk. "She didn't commit any damn crimes," he said.

The preacher halted, looked startled for a moment, gathered himself and went on. "The Lord giveth and the Lord taketh away," he said.

Fargo's voice cut him off. "And he smites the wicked for damn sure," he rasped.

The banker stepped forward, puffed himself up with pomposity. "You, sir, are interrupting a service," he said.

"I'm interrupting something that stinks," Fargo shot back.

The mayor decided to add his voice. "You're that friend of Nellie Noonan that's come here with all kinds of strange notions. I heard about you," he said. "You take your crackpot ideas someplace else."

42

"You'd like that, I'll bet," Fargo said.

"I'll not let you interrupt a solemn ceremony," the banker said. "Go on with it, Preacher."

"Dust to dust, ashes to ashes," the preacher said in a voice that quavered.

"Paying to paying, truth to truth," Fargo boomed out.

"Close it up, Seth," he heard Joe Holder call and the man began shoveling dirt at once. Fargo saw Joe Holder fasten Bonnie with a hard eye. "What are you doing here with him?" Holder asked her.

"Looking and listening," she shot back.

"You also lettin' him fill your head with fool ideas about your sister?" Holder said.

"I've my own ideas," Bonnie snapped. The man turned away but Fargo saw his sour face had taken on an ulcerous cast. He had sized up the undertaker as a lackey. Perhaps he was wrong, Fargo reflected. There was a dark danger behind the man's sour face. Holder returned to the hearse as the preacher climbed into the spring wagon with Mayor Smith and the banker. Fargo watched as the sheriff barked orders to two of his men.

"You're on till dark. Bert and Eddie will take night duty," the sheriff ordered, and the two men pulled rifles from their saddle holsters, dismounted and took up guard on both sides of the gravesite as the digger threw down the last mound of fresh earth.

"Little unusual, isn't it, post guard at the grave of a hung murderess," Fargo commented.

The mayor answered from the wagon. He had learned to be ready with smooth, prepared answers, Fargo saw, the hallmark of the lifelong politician, even in a backwater town such as Brushville. "We don't allow the desecration of our cemeteries. Some

43

folks are so angry at the killing of Judge Counsil that they might just do that," Smith said. "The judge being as popular as he was. You ought to be pleased we go to such lengths."

"Pleased as a pig in a mudhole," Fargo said, and saw Mayor Smith catch the sarcasm in his tone, turn back and snap the reins with his jaw grown rigid. The wagon rolled on and Joe Holder drove the hearse after it, his face still dark and full of sour simmering. Sheriff Coleman and the other horsemen rode alongside the hearse and Fargo turned the pinto and headed in the other direction. He tossed a last glance at the men standing guard beside the graveyard.

Bonnie rode beside him. "You didn't believe Tim Smith, did you?" she asked.

"He's a damn liar," Fargo bit out.

"Looks as though you won't be doing much digging up," Bonnie bit out. "They've shut the door on that idea."

"Patience, girl," Fargo muttered.

"Patience?" Bonnie frowned. "For what?"

"You ask too many questions," he said.

"I've a lot more."

"Save them till I get back."

"Where are you going?" She frowned again.

"To town, talk to people, find out exactly how popular this Judge Counsil was," he said.

"I can tell you that. He was the circuit judge, the town recorder, head of the Land Deeds Office, chief assayer and just about everything else. He was popular because he was the most powerful man in town. It paid to like Judge Counsil."

"How come you know so much for only having been here a little while?" Fargo asked.

44

"Carrie used to tell me things when she got drunk or down and Carrie knew a lot," Bonnie answered.

"I'm still going in and ask for myself," Fargo said.

"Why, dammit. That's wasting time."

"No it isn't. I want it known I'm asking questions, poking, prying, ferreting. I want to stir things up, flush the skunks out of their holes."

"And get yourself killed."

"That's been tried before. You worried about me?" He grinned.

"I thought two of us working together could do more," she muttered.

"We will. Patience, I told you. Just sit tight till I get back. I'll see you later at your place."

She moved her horse forward but he saw no concession in her face, her round cheeks even rounder as she glowered. She sent the horse into a fast, angry canter and he watched her breasts bounce delightfully against the lemon-yellow shirt as she rode away. He turned the Ovaro and cut across the field of wild bergamot, headed back toward Brushville. He rode with his lips drawn back, Bonnie's angry face in his mind, and he veered suddenly, crossed the field into a stand of shadbush and disappeared into the trees. He dismounted and let the pinto graze on a bed of white-flowered sweetclover. He leaned back against a tree and waited. Not more than a half-hour had gone by when he saw the horse moving fast across the field, the lemon-yellow shirt striking against the background of the pink and light magenta bergamots. He squinted, saw that she had the big Spencer pushed into a long saddle holster and he let her go by, waited, then pulled himself onto the pinto and followed, staying back. He'd made a wager with himself and wasn't happy that he'd won. "Stubborn little package," he muttered silently.

She moved out of sight for a few minutes and he swung the pinto in a half-circle, came over the small hillock and into view of the cemetery. She was there, halted at one side, the big Spencer in her hands, leveled at the two guards. She'd gotten the drop on them easily enough as they'd let her come close, not expecting she'd dare challenge them. Fargo moved the pinto through a line of trees and heard one of the men talk to her, his voice carrying clear in the stillness. "One of us would get you, girlie," the man said, an almost amused tolerance in his tone. "Now you just put that old rifle down."

"One of you is a dead man unless you start digging," Fargo heard Bonnie answer as he swung from the saddle and moved through the trees on silent footsteps.

"Sort of a Mexican standoff, I guess," the man said. "Besides, we don't have a shovel."

Fargo saw Bonnie in the saddle, her back to him through the trees, the Spencer still leveled at the two men. His glance shifted a fraction as he saw the narrow figure creeping up on her from the rear, the long-handled shovel held upraised. Fargo raced forward with the big Colt in his hand as he saw Seth bring the shovel around in a high arc, smash it into Bonnie's back. The Spencer went off harmlessly into the air as Bonnie pitched forward out of the saddle and Fargo heard her short cry of pain. He was at the edge of the trees as the two guards dived, one pouncing on her.

"My back . . . oooh," she gasped.

"You're gonna be yellin' about how sore your little pussy is when we're done with you, girlie," Fargo heard the man snarl, saw him fall onto Bonnie, tear his trousers open. He was pushing her legs apart and yanking at her riding britches as Seth came closer, his sunken eyes aglow with a strange light as he made short, stabbing motions with the handle of the shovel. Fargo halted, the Colt .45 raised. It would be easy to blow away the three of them, he thought as his finger poised on the trigger. But it wasn't time for killing, not yet. There was always time for that if it had to be. Pain was enough for now, pain and fear and anxiety. If there was payment due, he wanted the right ones to pay, not merely some hired hand. He shifted the Colt, gauged angles and heard the man atop Bonnie gurgling with lust. "Look here what I got for you, sweetie." The man laughed, lifting himself over her.

Fargo's shot grazed the right side of his temple with a painful, searing scrape of hot lead. "Ow, Jesus," the man shouted as he fell to one side, rolled on the ground. The second guard drew his gun but Fargo's shot blew it out of his hand and he fell backward in pain and surprise. Fargo saw the movement to his right, Seth coming at him with the shovel upraised. He fired again, directly at the shovel. The bullet hit with a loud, pinging sound, almost point-blank, and drove the shovel into Seth's face. The man toppled backward as the shovel fell from his hands, his face bleeding from cuts on both his eyebrows and on his cheekbones.

Fargo swung the six-gun back at the two guards. One pressed a kerchief to his temple, stared at the big man before him. The other was held by fear while Seth lay on the ground and made small, whimpering noises. "I don't want to have to kill anybody," Fargo said. "Don't do anything stupid."

He reached down with one hand, helped lift Bonnie to her feet as the Colt stayed trained on the two guards. "My back . . ." she gasped.

"Can you ride?" he asked.

"I'll ride," she said, pulling angry determination into her voice, but he heard the pain in her short breaths as she clambered onto the horse. He called out and the Ovaro trotted from the trees. He mounted without taking his gun from the two men though they were more than content to stay quiet.

"I'm going to let you boys off easy, with your skins in one piece," he said. "We'll just go on, now. You can consider yourselves damn lucky."

He turned the pinto, took the reins of Bonnie's mount and held it close to his own horse as he moved into the trees. His glance at Bonnie was harsh but he saw her throw anger back through her pain. "You've a hearing problem?" he said. "I told you to sit tight till I got back."

"I was getting you that answer you wanted," she snapped.

"You got yourself a sore back and almost a lot more," he grunted.

"Dammit, you said knowing if Nellie Noonan was inside that box was the first thing. You changed your mind?" she flung at him.

"You know better than that," he growled.

"No, I don't. Then why didn't you follow through, make them dig it up?" she pressed, the pain in her eyes not all from her sore back.

"I want the answer but I don't want them knowing I have it," Fargo said. "Not anymore, not till I get a better lead on what's going on around here. I don't want them covering up more. I want them thinking I'm still poking, wondering." Bonnie turned away, took in his reply but the glower stayed on her plump-cheeked prettiness. "That doesn't excuse your fat-headed move," Fargo rasped. "Went right against what I told you to do." She continued to glower as they drew up in front of the house. "You pull that kind of stunt again and you're on your own, you hearing me?" Fargo said.

She nodded and he saw her grimace with pain as she slid from the horse. He dismounted, held on to her arm as she took slow steps to the house. "The end of that damn shovel caught me right in the back muscles," she breathed. He held her inside the house till she reached the bedroom door, shook away his hand at her elbow. "I'll be all right," she said, her voice tight.

"Hell, you will," Fargo grunted. "You lay down, take that shirt off. I'll be right back with something that'll help."

He strode outside to the pinto, rummaged in his saddlebag to come out with a small, clay crock with a cork stopper. He returned to the house to find her on the bed lying on her stomach, but the lemon-yellow shirt still on. She turned her head to look at the small crock in his hand. "What's that?" she muttered.

"Oil of cajeput with fresh comfrey root and fresh columbine root. You'll be good as new come morning," he said. "I told you to take that shirt off."

"You'd use any excuse, wouldn't you?" she snapped.

"You going to take it off or do I?"

She stayed pressed down on the bed as she wriggled one arm out of the shirt, then the other and he lifted the garment away, tossed it aside. He took in nice shoulder, tanned and round, a slender, well-muscled back, tanned except for a band of white that

49

stretched across the lower part. He sat on the edge of the bed as he began to apply the ointment. Her skin was smooth, soft, exciting to the touch and he had to force himself to keep his mind on the task. He massaged firmly yet gently and her small gasps were made of both pain and pleasure. His strong fingers massaged and kneaded, working the oil through the pores of her skin. She'd hit the ground falling forward, landed on her right shoulder. It had to be bruised, as well.

"Turn over," he said. "You're going to need some of this on your shoulders."

"Turn over? Absolutely not."

"Come on. Believe me, I've seen bigger and better," he said with impatience.

Her head rose, turned to cast a glare at him. "Bigger, I'm sure, but not better." She lifted herself and pulled the sheet up over her breasts as she turned, allowing him only a glimpse of the side of one soft curve of flesh. She held the sheet covering herself as he massaged, his big hands encompassing each shoulder. Finally, finished, he stoppered the bottle and stood up.

"It works quickly. You'll feel better soon."

"I'm feeling better already, all warm and kind of tingly." Her eyes stayed on him as he started from the room. "Where are you going?"

"Find a place to spend the night."

"You can stay here. There's plenty of room," she said quickly. "And I've those questions to ask yet."

His eyes met her glance. She could be part little girl, part woman, he saw. "Why not?" He shrugged. "I'll unsaddle the horses and be back."

He went outside, tethered both horses and removed their gear. When he returned to the house, she was sitting up in bed, the sheet pulled up around her, pressed tight against the two modest mounds that pushed hard against it. She gestured to the top drawer of the old dresser. "There's a bottle of bourbon in there, if you've a mind," she said.

"I've a mind." He nodded, found the bottle and a shot glass and poured it full with the dark amber liquid. "You partial to bourbon?"

"Carrie was," she said. "And I've a taste for it."

He offered her the glass and she took a long sip from it, drew in breath as the whiskey burned its way with fiery warmth down her throat. Fargo raised the shot glass in salute, downed the rest of it. "To old Elijah Craig," he said.

"Who's he?" Bonnie frowned.

"A good Baptist clergyman who also made the first bottle of bourbon down Kentucky way," Fargo said. "I heard he was better at brewin' than baptizing." He poured another sip and Bonnie took it, her brown eyes serious and round.

"Thanks, Fargo," she said softly.

"For the bourbon or the rubdown?" he asked.

"For everything. I should've listened to you," she said, and he nodded in agreement. "I know, patience. But you're not going to tell me for what?"

"When the time comes."

She leaned back, regarded him with thoughtful, grave eyes. "When that time comes, what if it *is* Nellie Noonan?"

"There'll be paying to be done," he said quietly.

"You're so sure Nellie Noonan didn't kill Judge Counsil. Why? Don't you think she could've had an affair with him? People change, you know."

"She could've had an affair, I don't deny that," Fargo said. "But she wouldn't have killed him over it. Not Nellie."

"How can you be so damn sure?" Bonnie frowned.

"Because Nellie Noonan couldn't kill anyone. It was impossible for her." He took another draw of the bourbon. "Once, in Utah, she had a little eight-year-old niece, Tammy. Nellie was baby-sitting with the little girl one day when a bastard named Carswall came onto her and decided to have the two of them. Nellie put up a fight but he knocked her out and took the little niece, first. He was just finishing when Nellie woke. She flew at him like a she-bear with cubs and he smashed her down again and took her too. He'd taken his pants and gun belt off and when he finished, she grabbed his gun. That's when I happened by. She was pointing it right at him. She could have killed him with one shot. There was no way she could miss. I looked at her bruised face, her near-naked body and the naked little girl. I told her to shoot but she shook her head and let the gun drop. I'll always remember how she said, *'I can't, I can't. I can't kill . . . I can't.'* It was part of her, locked inside her, part the way she was brought up, part her own self. The bastard grabbed for his gun and I did what she couldn't do, blew his damn head off."

Fargo paused, his eyes seeing another time, another place. He finished the bourbon still in the glass, drew a deep breath. "I took Nellie home that day. The little girl never got over it. She became a recluse, wouldn't talk or see anyone, afraid of her own shadow. Doctors gave up on helping her, finally, said her mind had snapped. Nellie made taking care of that little girl her life. I'd send her money from time to time to help out. Five years later, the little girl just seemed to wither away and died. Nellie left Utah then and came here to Brushville, started a new life for herself."

Bonnie's voice was almost a whisper, hushed awe in it. "If she couldn't kill then, over that, she wouldn't kill over an affair gone sour," she said.

"You've got it," Fargo growled. "That's where somebody made a mistake. They didn't know that about Nellie Noonan."

Bonnie stayed silent for a long spell and he saw her brows knit as she searched for words. "If it isn't Nellie Noonan," she began. "If it's somebody else," she said, and he heard the break in her voice.

"If it's Carrie," he said, and she nodded, eyes down.

"Won't change anything. There'll still be paying to do."

Her brown eyes were deep and round as her arms lifted, encircled his neck. "Thanks," she murmured. Her lips parted, pressed against his mouth, sweetclover warmth and he felt the very tip of her tongue come forward to touch his mouth.

"Just saying thanks?" he asked.

She shrugged. "There's thanking and there's wanting. I don't know where one starts and the other stops."

He felt the sheet slip away from her as her arms tightened around his neck. Her lips opened wider and he closed one hand over a bare shoulder, pushed gently and she lay back on the bed. The sheet lay where it had slipped, just below her waist and he let his eyes savor the twin mounds, deeply tanned ex-

53

cept for the white, narrow band that began at the very top of her nipples. Still modest, her breasts nonetheless swelled with a soft curve, grew round and full quickly, tiny light pink tips in the center of deep pink circles, a soft fullness at the sides, rising with full-fleshed firmness.

"Maybe you're right, about bigger but not better," he murmured as his lips closed around one tiny pink tip.

"Ah . . . ah . . . ah, Jeez," he heard her breathe. Her hands closed around his neck, pulled on him. "No . . . I don't want . . . oh, God," she whispered, words trailing off to a sharp gasp, and he felt the shudder course through her as his tongue circled the tiny pink tip, his lips closing over it, moistening, licking. The little tip grew in his mouth, not so much in size as in firmness, and he felt her hands slip down to his chest as he pushed the shirt from his shoulders.

"Slow . . . please . . . slow," she murmured as she turned in his arms, protest, almost despair in her voice.

He pulled his mouth from her breast, held his lips poised over the softly firm flesh. "I'll stop if you want," he said, flicked his tongue across the very tip of the light pink nipple. She pushed herself upward almost angrily, her hand lifting her breast, parting his lips with the creamy softness. He closed his mouth, sucked, pulled her deep into him and she almost screamed. His hand moved, pushed her riding britches down and she raised her legs as if to help, kicked the garment free, used her hand to pull away pink bloomers. Her legs rose at once, together, firm and tanned with lovely, long thighs that rose to a

54

surprisingly plump little rear and a triangle that lay flat with tight, black curls.

He let his mouth move down across her abdomen, his tongue tracing an incandescent little trail down over her slightly convex tummy, down to the edges of the black, tight little curls. "Ah . . . ah . . . aiiiieee . . ." she gasped, and her hand pressed against him, closed, opened, searched with feverish haste and closed around his swollen, throbbing maleness. "Oh, my God, my God . . . oh, please, yes, do it, do it . . . oh, Jesus, Fargo . . . do it," he heard her moan, words running into each other without pause between. His hand found its way through the flat, curly hair, pressed against the soft mound under it and her tanned legs fell open, straightened, quivered as they stretched out and the quivering took over the rest of her body. He came onto her, rested the powerful potency of his maleness against her fleshy pubic mound and felt her belly suck in as he pulled her hips back and upward, as the lock seeks the key. He slid into her with deliberate slowness, felt the hot tightness of her give, stretch, the inner trembling that massaged him with maddening pleasure. Bonnie pulled back again as if to draw him further and he moved with her, thrust inward and heard her short, harsh scream and then her legs rose, clamped around the small of his back, the eternal vise of pleasure.

He moved with her wrapped around him, felt the plump underside of her rear touch the back of his legs, slid forward slowly, back, forward again and the tightness of her stayed around him, a warm embrace of the flesh and he heard her tiny half-whimpering, half-imploring sounds. A word took form, shape, spiraled from her as he felt her belly draw in again. "Now ... now ... now ..." Bonnie cried out, and her body began to tremble and he felt her tighten around him outside and inside. The sensation drew him forward, sending him into quick, hard thrusts and Bonnie screamed out with each one as she pushed upward for more. He felt the frantic haste seize him as it had her, a cry from the flesh, beyond all will, beyond all control, the tyranny of ecstasy. He thrust fully into her and she screamed, dug fingernails into his back and he was oblivious to the pain of it. "Yes, yes, damn, damn ... yes," Bonnie screamed, and moved convulsively under him. His mouth bent down, closed around one firm breast as she put her head back and the wail was not unlike that of a she-wolf he'd once heard high in the timberland, a cry of overwhelming beauty and terrible aloneness, triumph and despair put together into one long, paean.

It was almost a minute before he felt her legs relax, fall away from his back and the warm softness encircling him grew limp. He pulled slowly from her as she made tiny sounds of unhappiness and he lay on his stomach beside her, watched her eyes blink open, take a moment to focus. "It's been a long time for you," Fargo said. "Or maybe never."

She shrugged. "I told you, Carrie was always the wild one. There was a time, too long ago." She rose on her elbows and her breasts lifted, pointed upward with magnificent, firm fullness and her eyes studied him. "I don't know why now, all of a sudden, why I wanted so much," Bonnie murmured. "Maybe everything that's happened making me all wound up inside. Maybe you and the way you look at a woman, everything put together."

"You sorry?" he asked.

She paused, shook her head. "No," she said. "Not sorry, just surprised at myself."

"It happened. Let it stay at that."

"Still makes me wonder why."

"Wondering about why only cuts into enjoying," he told her.

She lay back, her lips pursed in thought for a moment, then reached arms up to encircle his neck. She pulled him down over her soft-firm breasts and he felt her move the little light pink tips back and forth against his skin, a tingling sensation. "No more wondering," she murmured, opened her lips and waited for his mouth. He pressed down onto her warm, wet waiting, harbinger of other lips. He felt the tiny tips grow firmer under his chest, traced a small line of warmth down her throat, over her collarbone, down over the tanned mounds, found the nipples, moved from one to the other, sucking, caressing, licking. Bonnie's breath grew shallower, her tiny gasps longer and her felt her legs move, lift upward, turn to him and her murmured words were only flesh given sound. "Please . . . oh, Jeez, Fargo . . . oh, Jeez . . . yes, yes, yes," he heard her breathe, and then the sharp, half-laugh, half-cry of ecstasy as he slid into her.

The night moved into its own deepness, surrounded Fargo with dark as Bonnie surrounded him with warm wetness until at last she lay alongside him, asleep in his arms and he looked down at her, half smiled in wonder as she was able to look sweet and sensuous at once, sleep stripping away all other pretenses. He settled down, closed his eyes and let weariness push aside all the questions without answers that gave reason for his presence beside Bonnie. They'd all wait for morning, he knew, ready to leap forward again, beggars of the mind demanding to be fed.

3

Fargo watched Sheriff Coleman follow him with his eyes as he dismounted and draped the Ovaro's reins over a hitching post in the center of town. He'd ridden slowly past the sheriff's office and saw the man emerge at once, watch him proceed leisurely up Brushville's main street. The sheriff's frown had been one of instant concern, his mouth becoming a thin slit across his face. Fargo stretched, began to saunter along the street, his every move planned, considered carefully.

He'd left Bonnie still looking delicious in the old bed. "What are you going to do?" she had asked with a glower as he had strapped on his gun belt.

"What I didn't get to do yesterday," he said pointedly, and the glower deepened. "Stir things up, make them uncomfortable. You stay here and wait this time, you hearing me?"

"Loud and clear," she snapped, and he waited, his eyes on her as she continued to glower at him. Her lips straightened finally and she blinked at him. "I promise," she said, and he nodded acceptance as he left the house. He'd skirted the cemetery on the Ovaro. Two guards were there, two different ones, but he'd expected that. These two were cut of the same cloth as the other two, hired hands, bored, waiting only for the chance to spend their pay. He'd ridden on to Brushville and he felt the grimness inside him, masked with a casual manner as he halted at a cooper's little shop. The man bent a long, narrow hoop of wood, nodded to the big, black-haired man that leaned in his doorway.

"Can I help you, stranger?" the cooper asked as he fitted the big hoop around a wide-bellied barrel.

"Hope so," Fargo said pleasantly. "Got some questions, about the Nellie Noonan hanging."

"What kind of questions?" the cooper asked as he continued at his work.

"About what folks thought. You believe she shot Judge Counsil?" Fargo kept his voice even.

He watched the wariness slide across the cooper's face. "No reason not to. Wasn't there to see for myself."

"Most folks here feel that way?" Fargo asked casually.

"Most," the cooper said. "What makes you so interested, stranger?"

"I knew Nellie Noonan. I don't believe she did it," Fargo answered. "But I appreciate your talking to me," he added as the man shrugged noncommittally. He walked on to the barber shop, two men and the barber inside, one in the chair, the other waiting. Fargo pushed the door open and went inside but not before he saw Sheriff Coleman heading for the cooper's shop.

"Fifteen-minute wait, mister," the barber said as Fargo entered the shop. A bald-headed, small man, he took in the big black-haired man with instant respect.

"Want some answers, not a haircut," Fargo said, keeping his voice casual. The barber paused, shears held open at the back of the man's neck in the barber chair. "Came here about Nellie Noonan. I don't buy it that she killed Judge Counsil." Fargo's eyes moved around the small shop. The man waiting picked up a raggedy newspaper and began poring through it, concentrating fiercely. The barber's shears clacked determinedly as he bent to his work and the man in the chair stared into space. "You folks all believe she did it?" Fargo pressed.

"They caught her red-handed," the barber muttered.

"So I hear," Fargo said. "Anybody know for sure if she and the judge were having an affair?"

"Knew they were friends," the barber said.

Fargo's glance moved across the other two men. "You gents any opinions?"

The man in the chair sat up straight, flung words out with sudden vehemence. "It's done with. Leave it at that, I say. Can't change anything now."

Fargo let reluctance tinge his smile. "I like knowing the truth," he said. "Guess I'll just have to keep trying to find it. See you around." He left with a polite nod, stepped into the street and walked on, satisfied at how it was going. He stopped at the blacksmith's and the general store, whose owner, a thin, reedy man, barely spoke to him when he began his questioning. When he left the store, he headed for the saloon, glancing back to see Sheriff Coleman, like a furtive shadow, following in his footsteps.

Fargo went into the saloon and saw the bartender recognize him at once, his face growing impassive as he poured the bourbon. Fargo took the drink to a table, sat down, started conversations with those who sat nearby as the bartender watched and listened. The man wasn't a part of anything, Fargo was certain, his aim simply to stay in the sheriff's good graces and so he'd be eager to report everything he could. Fargo kept his voice raised to make sure the man would miss nothing. But the pattern held, and he'd expected as much, his questions and assertions met with caution, evasiveness or silence. No conspiracy, he had already concluded, just human nature at work, people anxious to look away, afraid of trouble, not without care, only without courage.

But he continued to bait one saloon customer after another and only an old man, with eyes that had long stopped caring about the world, offered anything. "They were good friends, the judge and Nellie Noonan," he said in response to one of Fargo's probes. "Saw them together lots. She helped the judge with his record keeping."

"What was the judge like?" Fargo questioned.

"Tall, gray hair, about fifty years on him," the old man said. "He was a tough judge, took in the whole circuit."

"You know Nellie?"

"Just to say hello," the old man answered. "Never seemed the kind for shooting people but you can't ever tell with women." The old man turned to his drink and drew into himself. He'd say nothing more, Fargo knew, and let his eyes flick to the bartender as he rose, his last question saved for the man.

"Nellie Noonan had a piece-goods store. Where is it?" he asked.

"On up the street," the bartender said. "Sheriff padlocked the place. Didn't want any looting."

"He's a fine man, the sheriff," Fargo commented as he walked from the saloon. Outside, he retrieved the Ovaro, led the horse by a loose rein as he walked up the street, moving slowly, leisurely. The sheriff would be inside the saloon by now, he guessed as he halted outside a narrow store with a drawn window shade, a heavy padlock on the door. He stood staring at it for a few minutes before moving on, paused at a watering trough and let the Ovaro drink his fill. He halted when he reached the end of town, examined the horse's hooves, adjusted the stirrups, tightened the cinch and found a patch of witchgrass and let the horse graze. Finally, enough time used up, he turned back and began to saunter through town again. He held the grim smile inside himself as he saw Sheriff Coleman advance toward him when he reached the center of town.

"Hold it there, Fargo," the sheriff said. "Some people want to talk to you."

"Me?" Fargo echoed and let himself seem surprised.

"You've been going all over town trying to stir up trouble about the Nellie Noonan hanging," the sheriff said.

"Just asking questions. No law against that, is there?" Fargo said mildly.

"You're upsetting folks." The sheriff frowned.

"Tough shit." Fargo smiled affably.

"The mayor and Charley Evans want to talk to you," the sheriff said. "They're very bothered about the things you've been saying. Don't mind telling you that I am, too." He started to turn, halted as he saw the big, black-haired man hadn't moved. "You coming?"

"You asking or ordering?" Fargo said softly but blue ice coated his eyes. He watched Sheriff Coleman wet his lips, wrestle with himself and saw caution, perhaps fear, win out over anger.

"Asking," the sheriff muttered.

"Then I'll be happy to oblige." Fargo smiled pleasantly and followed as the sheriff crossed the street to the bank. Inside, past the single teller's window with a brass grille, the sheriff halted at a closed door, knocked authoritatively and Fargo saw the door open.

"Got Fargo with me," the sheriff said. The door opened wider and Fargo saw the banker, Mayor Smith behind him.

"Come in," Evans said, and Fargo stepped into the inner office, a proper banker's office richly furnished with a fine, polished mahogany desk, three big stuffed chairs and steel engravings on the walls. The banker gestured to one of the stuffed chairs.

"I'll stand," Fargo said.

The banker shrugged, went around behind his desk and seated himself. Mayor Smith stood nearby, the sheriff to one side.

"It appears you're under a set of very wrong impressions," Evans began, his tone almost unctuous. Fargo felt himself bristle.

"Such as?" he clipped out.

"Those things you've been saying ever since you came to town," the banker said. "That's why we wanted to talk with you. Perhaps we can put your mind at ease about this entire sorry affair."

"I'd like that," Fargo said blandly.

Evans smiled, gathered instant confidence. "You sailed into town full of wild accusations and you've been unfair to everyone involved," he said. "Nellie Noonan was caught with the gun still in her hand. Sheriff Coleman had just arrived at the judge's office when he heard the shot, ran in and saw her with the gun."

"Just the sheriff?" Fargo queried.

64

"No, I was with him," the mayor cut in. "I saw her too."

"Two eyewitnesses, two of our most respected citizens, Fargo," the banker said. "And she confessed all the rest when she was brought in, about the affair and how Judge Counsil wanted out, all of the sordid story. I'm afraid your long friendship with Nellie Noonan just led you into a pack of wrong conclusions."

"Perhaps we were hasty in the hanging, but our reasons have already been explained to you," Mayor Smith put in. "That's got nothing to do with her guilt."

Fargo's glance moved from one man to the other. They were all brazening it out, all committed to the same story. "Open the box. Let me see Nellie in it," he said.

"Dammit, you've your nerve, Fargo," the banker exploded. "That's as much as saying you don't believe a word of what we've told you."

"Seems that way, doesn't it? Open the box," Fargo said.

The mayor's voice cut in. "We can't do that. That takes a court order around here. Judge Counsil could've issued that. It'll take at least a month to get one from a judge in Clinton. Ironic, isn't it?"

"Ironic bullshit, that's what it is," Fargo flung back.

"Now see here, Fargo, we've had enough of you, your crazy suspicions and your unfounded accusations," Evans shouted. "We thought a proper explanation would satisfy you. It seems we were mistaken. But we won't stand for any more loose talk, accusations and innuendos. Take your damn wild ideas and get out of town."

Fargo chose words carefully. He wanted to tell them just enough to let them know he wasn't buying, nothing else, not yet. He needed to know more before shoving their mistake down their throats. "I'll leave," he said, caught the banker's moment of relief. "When I get the damn answers I want," he finished, spun and started for the door.

"Fargo!" the sheriff called, and the big man stopped with one hand on the doorknob, looked back at the three men. "I could lock you up as a troublemaker," the sheriff threatened.

"You could try," Fargo said, his voice velvet over steel. He turned as the sheriff swallowed, pushed the door open and strode from the bank. Outside, he mounted the Ovaro, sent the horse leisurely down the street and out of town. The day was winding itself down. It had gone almost exactly as he'd expected it to go. So far he'd been right on target. His probing and prying had brought the words; at first, smooth words, prepared explanations, then the warnings and threats when he had stayed adamant. And now it was time for the next move. That would have been given over to Sheriff Coleman and the man would have prepared by now. The sheriff had been around long enough to know trouble when he saw it and Fargo remembered how the man had read his eyes when they'd first met.

Fargo grunted as he rode from town and steered away from Bonnie's place as the shadows grew long. He'd not bring this down on her too. He rode slowly, took the Ovaro across the low hills with the open spaces and heavily wooded stands of aspen and balsam, oak and hemlock with thick undergrowth of shrubs, mostly snowberries and hollyleaf buckthorn. He climbed a narrow trail between tall, thick balsams, halted to slide from the saddle at a spot where he could peer out between the branches. His eyes slowly traveled across the hills and the tiny smile that edged his lips held bitterness in it. The foliage at the left moved with the progressive, steady movement caused by men on horseback. On the right, the same telltale sign and on ahead, up hill of where he was, the quick movement of leaves and branches. One, maybe two riders, he guessed. His lips pursed. They had been positioned, waiting, watching. The sheriff had made his moves quickly, professionally, taking no chances. He'd plainly given instructions to watch and wait and go into action if they saw the Ovaro ride from town.

Fargo pulled himself back onto his horse. They had watched him go into the trees, spread out, and now he'd let them see him again, let him think he was totally unaware, blithely confident. He moved the pinto out into the clear space alongside the trees, rode slowly, stayed in the open until the light grew dim. He turned into the trees then, and knew they'd be watching. Inside the woods, he picked a small clear spot as the night turned the forest into inky blackness. He positioned the Ovaro where he couldn't be missed later, left his bedroll against a tree not far from the horse. He lay down in the blackness and catnapped. It would be a waiting game for a few hours, until the moon rose high enough to let its pale light sift down through the trees and turn the forest into a place of pale silver and shadow.

He rested, napped, woke and pulled himself to his feet while the woods were still pitch black. The moon would sift its light down soon and they'd start to converge on him, a three-pronged pincer movement, from both sides and the top. They'd come carefully but feeling securely confident. Were they not the hunters, the pursuers? Fargo's lips pulled back tightly.

He had all but set it up that way, had anticipated and been right once again. Now it was time to turn the hunters into the hunted. He began to move north through the blackness, steps soundless as a lynx on the prowl. The two at the top of the pincers, first. Taking them out would cut away one-third of the pincer and not only reduce the odds but change the picture. The others would come in, wait, wonder, and coordination would vanish. He moved almost on hands and knees, feeling his way through the pitch blackness and straightened as tiny glimmers of silver light began to touch the leaves. Trees and branches began to take on shadowed shapes.

The terrain rose and he pulled himself up, straining his eyes. He paused, sniffed the air, his eyes narrowing as he took in the hint of dampness. He moved forward, estimated that he had another fifteen minutes before the moonlight brightened the forest, more than enough time to turn these two hunters into the hunted. He moved forward, drew a deep breath and froze. His nostrils took in the smell of leather, but too strong, too close. He stiffened as the two shapes took form directly in front of him, only a few feet away, both on foot, both holding rifles.

"Goddamn," he swore as the one figure raised his rifle, dropped onto his haunches and felt the black of the rifle knock his hat off. He dived forward, slammed into the man at knee level and the figure went down on its back. Fargo brought his fist around in a hammerlike blow into the man's belly and heard the cursed gasp of air. He started to yank the Colt from its holster, had it in his hand when he saw the shadowed shape of the second man leaping at him with both feet outstretched. Fargo tried to twist but the man was too close and his heels came down across the Trailsman's back. Fargo felt the pain shoot down his spine and his right arm go limp. He felt the Colt slide from his suddenly soft fingers, skitter over the man on the ground and disappear into the brush. The figure that had leaped on him had landed on one knee, turned, started to bring his rifle around. Fargo rolled from the man below him who still clutched his belly with one hand, heard the rifle blast a shot over his head. He rolled back, into the second man's legs, wrapped one arm around an ankle and yanked. The man toppled backward with a curse.

Fargo twisted away, the limpness in his right arm starting to lessen, and he dove into the brush, rolled, came up behind the thick trunk of a balsam. He stayed motionless as a frog on a lily pad and swore silently, mostly at himself. The two men had taken him by surprise. They'd been moving down just as he'd been on the move upward, for the same reasons, to move in before the moon rose further. They had planned to take the same advantage he'd wanted for himself. His own fault, he swore again at himself. He'd underestimated them and to underestimate was always a mistake. These two, at least, were a cut above the average. The others had of course heard the shots. They'd be moving in from both sides.

He reached down and drew the narrow, razor-sharp knife from the leg holster around his right calf. Double-edged, called by some an Arkansas toothpick, it was a perfectly balanced throwing knife. Without his gun, he had to lessen the odds quickly. He let his arm hang, felt the limpness disappearing from it as the bruised nerve regained its strength. The two men were playing the same game again, staying silent, and he'd accorded them a grim kind of respect. But suddenly the sound of brush being pushed aside broke the silence, grew louder, came from both his right and his left. Fargo almost smiled as he took a firmer grip on the knife. He waited, certain of what would happen and he smiled as the voice called out.

"Hang back," one of the men shouted. "We've got him here. Make a circle, case he gets by us."

The voice had come from behind a pair of oaks now outlined in the pale moon's glow. Fargo moved on the balls of his feet, crouched low, staying behind the thick brush, a soundless wraith in the night. He made a half circle, came up behind the figure by the two oaks. The man had his rifle raised, ready to fire and Fargo's eyes moved past the figure to find the second man lying almost prone, the rifle propped up on top of a log, his shoulder to the stock. Fargo's eyes returned to the figure behind the oaks. He raised the blade, aimed, knotted powerful shoulder muscles and the knife winged through the moon-tinted night. It hurtled into the back of the man's neck, halted only when the hilt embedded itself in flesh and the tip of the blade end protruded from the front of the figure's neck. The man stayed unmoving, and Fargo counted off seconds, squinted at the blade, wondered if the dark was playing tricks on him. He almost moved when the figure slowly toppled forward into the oaks, rested face against the bark, still, silent and strangely peaceful.

Fargo moved forward, halted, his hands groping carefully along the ground. His fingers touched coldness, smooth hardness and he picked up the rock, just large enough to hold in his big hand. He crept forward again, toward the figure lying in wait. He crept closer, drawing his breath in. The man continued to peer ahead into the forest. Fargo risked another step closer. The man suddenly lifted his head, started to turn, when the rock crashed into his forehead. He uttered a gasp of pain as he fell backward. Fargo leaped forward, reached the figure in seconds. The man had let the rifle fall from his hand and Fargo seized it, brought the heavy stock around and smashed it into the man's already bleeding forehead. He heard the crunch of shattered bone as the figure jerked convulsively on the ground and lay still.

"Sammy?" a voice shouted from the trees.

Fargo tightened his vocal cords, rasped out the words. "Got him. Come on in," he called. He slid back, moved around the trunk of an aspen, the rifle in his hands. He watched the forest move, the circle of figures begin to come forward. He counted four in one side of the pincer, three on the other. He chose the four, raised the rifle, waited a moment longer.

"Where the hell are you?" a voice called out.

"Here," Fargo murmured as he pulled the trigger, managed to get off three quick shots. He saw the nearest figure disappear and a scream of pain followed. The other two figures made only gargling noises as they went down. He heard the others diving for cover with shouted curses, used the noise they made to move from the aspen and flatten himself behind the brush. Four left, he muttered, and the rifle held only one more shot. He waited, his eyes moving back and forth across the night forest. A shape suddenly rose, darted from behind a tree. Fargo's shot was instant and he saw the shape vanish, the man's scream of pain turn into a long, sobbing sound until it finally died away into silence. Three,

71

Fargo muttered. The woods stayed silent for another few minutes and suddenly erupted in the frantic rustling of brush. The three remaining were crawling away on their bellies, three who wanted only to escape with their lives.

Fargo stayed in place and grimaced. He'd wanted to question one but there was no chance of that now. The sheriff would find out his plans had failed sooner or later. Now he'd learn a little sooner. Fargo shrugged, grunted. It didn't matter. What mattered was that the sheriff and the others become more nervous, more frightened, come closer to making another mistake. Fargo heard the sound of horses galloping away and he rose, slowly, cautiously, listened again. But the forest had grown silent with the stillness of death. He walked to the two oaks, pulled his throwing knife free and wiped it clean. He searched the forest floor for the Colt, the pale light little help in the thick brush. Almost twenty minutes passed before he found the gun and slipped it into its holster. His back hurt and he realized he was bleeding from a cut alongside his temple. He made his way to the Ovaro, winced as he pulled himself into the saddle. He rode back slowly as thoughts slid through his mind.

It had come full circle, words to convince him, first, then the bullets to put an end to his questions. And the reason still wore a shroud. Why, dammit, he mused. What did they fear he'd find out? They insisted they had hung Nellie Noonan. If so, it was with a strange, twisted noose.

He rode from the woods into a moonlit hillside, headed down into flat country and saw the light glimmering from Bonnie's house as he finally crossed the field of wild bergamot. She was in the doorway as he slid from the saddle, her plump cheeks wreathed in concern.

"Jesus, what happened to you?" she said as she hurried forward, put an arm around his waist, her eyes scanning his face.

"Tell you inside," he said.

"I'll get that ointment out of your saddlebag," Bonnie offered.

"Don't need it," he said. "Just a cold towel and some sleep." He went into the house as Bonnie stepped back, turned and unsaddled the pinto while he undressed to his shorts and stretched out on the old brass bed. She returned, sat down on the edge of the bed beside him.

"Damn, I was worried." She rested her head against his shoulder.

"That's nice to hear," he said. She rose, got a wet towel and cleaned the dried blood from the side of his temple. He told her all that had taken place from the moment he'd gone to Brushville in the morning. When he finished, she frowned at him.

"You practically brought it on yourself? Why?"

"Smoke them out, make them move out from behind their masks. I suspected and now I'm sure. The mayor, the banker and the sheriff, they're in it together, whatever it is. And maybe the undertaker. But I'm sure of the first three, now. They took the bait, acted and now I know that much for sure."

"Now what?" Bonnie asked.

He closed his eyes. "I get some sleep," he breathed.

"And tomorrow?"

He answered with his eyes closed. "Tomorrow we do some digging up. Now let me get some sleep."

He heard her hiss of surprise. "Why tomorrow, all of a sudden?" she pressed.

His eyes stayed shut. "A heavenly sign," he muttered.

"A what?"

"A heavenly sign. Good night," he said.

"Go to hell," she flung back angrily. He stayed unmoving, his eyes closed. He heard her stand up, fling off clothes and the bed dipped as she lay down beside him, her back to him. He felt the weariness flood through his body and he was almost asleep when she turned, nuzzled herself against him, one arm draped over his chest. She fell asleep with him that way.

She'd hardly moved when morning came and he opened his eyes, focused on the window. He grunted in satisfaction, slept another hour until he felt Bonnie stir, get up. He opened one eye, watched her tanned, lovely form, the plump little rear not really fitting the rest of her yet terribly appealing, as she slipped into a loose robe, took the heavy enameled pitcher with her and went outside. He was up when she returned with the pitcher full of well-water and he washed quickly. "It's starting to rain," she muttered.

"By dark it'll be a downpour," Fargo answered, and she frowned at him. "A heavenly sign, I told you."

"Why? What's that do for us?" She washed her face in the cold water.

"Those guards won't stay the night in a downpour. Soon as it gets dark they'll take off and hole up in some barn someplace," Fargo said. She dried her face and he saw the understanding in her eyes.

"We just wait around here for night," she said.

He reached out, flipped the robe open and curled

his palm under one firm breast. "It won't be exactly wasted time."

A tiny glimmer of satisfaction slid into her eyes. "Good," she murmured, pulled back from his touch, slid the robe from her shoulders and fairly leaped onto the bed. He dived after her and she grasped for him at once, gave a sharp little gasp as she felt him swelling, throbbing inside her palm. "Oh, Jeez . . . Jeez," Bonnie said and she swung her legs over him, pulled at him, pushed her dark portal onto him. He felt her eagerness but she was still dry, desire ahead of the flesh. He held back, pushed his mouth down over her breasts, pulled on them and she almost screamed. He spun her on her back, let his lips almost race down her belly, across the curled tightness of her little triangle. He let his tongue touch her, a quick flicking motion, then longer, slower. "Oh. Christ . . . iiiieee . . . oh, Jeez," Bonnie cried out, and instantly the dryness had vanished and he felt her flowing, lips warm and wet. He thrust into her quickly, almost harshly. "Ah . . . ah . . . aaagh . . . Jeez, oh, Christ yes, I want . . . oh, please, Fargo . . . Jeez," Bonnie flung out in staccato little bursts of breath. She rose under him, and his hands reached down, clasped hold of the plump rear, drew her up and pushed deep inside her, held the very tip of his pulsating organ against the soft wall of her warm darkness. He held there and she made little motions against him. "Oh . . . aaah . . . aaaaaaaah . . . oh, please, please, harder, please harder," she cried out, and he felt her legs tightening against him, pushing, trying to make him release her.

He did so, suddenly, unexpectedly and she screamed in pleasure and protest and he drew back, almost to the very edge of her lips. "No . . . Jesus, no," Bonnie called out, panic seizing her voice.

"No," he echoed, "no," and he plunged forward. Her scream became a garbled, almost gutteral sound as she gulped in air. He rode her, soft and then hard, slow and then fast and Bonnie's head turned and twisted against the bed and little sounds of ecstasy fell from her opened mouth. He brought her higher, felt her stomach tighten, let his own wanting explode within her as her hips rose, lifted and her legs clamped around his waist. She threw her head back, her breasts lifting and her hands pulled his face down into their tanned softness as she came with him, wonderful warmth of her inner being flooding around him as she cried little screams of pleasure.

"Jeez," she breathed as she sank back finally and his still throbbing thickness filled her with plethoric delight. "Stay . . . stay," she murmured, and he lay atop her, feeling the tight curls of her little black triangle against his belly. It was minutes before her legs fell open and she gave a shuddering sigh as he withdrew from her. She turned on her side against him and was asleep in seconds and he held her there, aware again of how she could be sweet and sensuous at once. He closed his eyes, slept with her as the rain grew harder against the roof of the house.

He woke later with a small warm sensation moving along his abdomen, looked down to see Bonnie's lips nibbling against his skin. He reached a hand down, touched her hair, and she moved her lips faster, as if afraid he'd hold her back. He felt the instant stirrings in his groin, the rising, thickening, pounding blood stirring at once. And then the wet warmth around him, drawing, circling, wondrously sweet pullings as Bonnie made tiny noises of pleasure. She stayed with him as he grew thicker, stronger, throbbing symbol of all that was between man and woman eternal and finally, with a triumphant cry, she pulled from him, brought her flowing portal onto him, sank down with a long groaning sound. She leaned over him, pushed the tanned, soft-firm breasts into his mouth as she pumped her plump little rear up and down on him. He felt her try to go slowly but her wanting caused her to spiral out of control and in moments she was half leaping, half smashing herself against him.

When the moment came, she dug knees deep into his sides and her scream came buried into his shoulder, her teeth fastening hard on his powerful muscles. "Ah . . . aaaah, Jeez," Bonnie breathed finally, pulling her teeth from him, flattening herself over him. Her arms encircled his neck and she nuzzled his ear with her lips and she made little wet sounds, almost little-girl sounds. She straightened her legs, her body across him, her face pressed into his chest. "You could be hard to leave, Fargo . . . too hard," she murmured. "Maybe, when this is over, you could stay here."

He stroked the tanned softness of her breasts, a gentle, soothing action this time. "Not likely, honey," he said. "Not likely."

"I've this house. It's Carrie's," she said. "You could stay on."

He pushed onto one elbow, smiled down at her. "You've this half a house," he corrected. "I've been meaning to ask you about that."

"A man Carrie went with built it, a carpenter. He was half finished when he took sick with the plague and died. Carrie wasn't about to finish it so it's still the way he left it," Bonnie explained.

Fargo swung from the bed and she followed, watched as his eyes went to the window. The rain was falling hard now, raindrops exploding as they struck the glass in the last light of the afternoon. "I've some cold chicken," she said. "I'll fix it with a little rice."

He nodded, doused himself with the water from the big pitcher and dried himself as Bonnie warmed the rice in an iron pot. He dressed, saw a tightness had come into her face and she said little as they ate, grew more silent as the night came and the rain continued to pound the window. "Got a shovel and a lantern here?" he asked.

"Someplace. Basement, maybe," she said. He started to rise. "I'll fetch them," she said, and there was a sullenness in her voice. He waited as she climbed down a few steps into what appeared to be really a basement. She reappeared holding a shovel and a kerosene lantern, set them down before him with her face tight.

"Second thoughts?" he asked, not ungently.

Her lips thinned and she lifted her eyes to his and he saw the pain in their brown depths. "I want to know, bad as you do, and I'm afraid to know," she said. "I want to and I don't want to. Crazy, isn't it?"

He drew her against him. "Not really. But I have to find out, you know." She nodded, lifted her face, kissed him gently, tenderly. He held her for another moment, peered over her hair to the rain pounding against the window. "Time to move," he said.

"I've a rainslicker," she said. "I'll bundle up." He left her, went to his gear and took out a gray poncho, donned it and became almost invisible beneath the garment. He saddled both horses and she came from the house with the lantern and the shovel. He took the shovel from her, mounted up and led the way from the house. She followed close at his heels. Rain pelted the tiny part of his face not covered and he lowered his head as the pinto made its way across the field and up the sloping, low hills. The night was pitch black and the rain drummed steadily, ocassionally whipped into bursts of fury by the wind.

He slowed as they crested the top of a hill. The cemetery had to be near, he knew, and he peered into the blackness, moved forward, halted again and Bonnie came up alongside him. "It's got to be just ahead of us but I don't want any light, not yet, not till I'm sure I figured right. You stay here." He dismounted and started forward on foot. He groped his way, careful steps, sliding his feet along the ground in the pitch blackness. He went forward again, stumbled as his foot hit against something hard. He fell forward, felt the smooth top of a headstone. He stayed motionless, listened and heard only the rain. He turned, made his way back the few yards to where Bonnie waited. "Light up," he said, and she took a moment but finally the flickering light glowed from the lantern. He took the lantern and handed her the big Sharps from its saddle holster. "You take this. You see anyone coming, you start shooting. Don't worry about hitting them. Just shoot and give me time to douse the light." She nodded, her face set. "I don't expect there'll be anyone coming," he added reassuringly.

He started forward through the cemetery, threaded his way past headstones to the far side where he halted beside the freshly dug dirt now rain-soaked and crumbly. He dug the shovel in, glanced up to see Bonnie standing back, barely visible in the dim glow of the lantern. "You tell me," she said.

His lips pursed. "I'll know if it's Nellie. What if it's somebody else?" he said.

"Carrie's got a birthmark over her collarbone," Bonnie said, and he turned, began to dig. The shovel went easily into the soft, wet earth and he dug steadily, doggedly. The rain drove with renewed fierceness against his face and made the lantern flicker with its force, as though nature protested his actions. He swore angrily at everything that had brought him to this place on this rain-swept night and he knew he was afraid of what he might find. Suddenly he understood Bonnie's feelings with the understanding that comes from the gut and not just the mind. He had a small mound of earth to one side when the shovel hit against solid wood. He stopped digging, carried the lantern closer to the hole and the light illuminated the front of the pine box.

Fargo took the shovel, pushed the edge under the lid and pried, heard the nails creak as they pulled free. A blast of rain hit into him and he wiped his eyes clear, pried again with the shovel as his lips drew back and he tried without success to shake the morbid feeling that rose inside him. A final pry with the shovel and he dropped to one knee, grasped the opened lid of the box with one hand and pulled. He stared through the rain into the narrow pine casket. The young woman inside seemed to stare back at him even though her eyes were closed.

He felt the words form soundlessly on his lips. *It's not Nellie*, he breathed. *It's not Nellie.* He felt Bonnie's eyes on him, looked up to peer through the downpour at her. Barely visible, she was a small shadow in the darkness but he knew her eyes were fixed on him. "It's not Nellie Noonan," he called out, and she made no sound. He swore softly and turned back to the box, reached down with one hand and fought away the wave of distaste that swept over him. The young woman wore a white blouse and he gently pulled one edge back, stared at a small, dark birthmark exactly over her left collarbone. "Goddamn," he breathed. "Goddamn the bastards."

He rose to his feet, walked to Bonnie. Her round eyes held on his face and her questions needed no asking. She came against him and he held her as the rain poured upon them. He pulled back, finally. "I'll hurry," he said as he returned to the opened grave, lowered the lid back onto the box and furiously began to shovel the dirt back into the hole. He finished, patted the earth down with the flat of the shovel, watched the rain make tiny rivulets along the soaked earth for a few moments and turned, strode back to Bonnie with the shovel and the lantern in his hands.

He left the lantern on until he led her from the cemetery and saw her in the saddle. He turned it out then and rode in silence beside her through the storming dark until, at last, the house came into view across the field, the light burning in the window. Bonnie went inside as he stabled the horses. When he entered, he heard her soft, bitter sobs from the bedroom and he let her alone with her grief. He found the bourbon, poured a drink for himself and sat down in the front room, let thoughts circle in his mind as though they were horses on a runaway carousel.

They hadn't hung Nellie Noonan. He wanted to seize on hope for that but didn't dare. She wasn't in that pine box but maybe she was just as lifeless someplace else. New questions whirled with new fury. They'd called Nellie a killer and hung her for all to see, only they'd hung Carrie Akins instead, with a sack over her head. But Judge Counsil had been killed, his burial open for all to see. Yet if they needed Nellie Noonan as a scapegoat, why didn't they simply follow through with her? Why hang Carrie Akins in her place? Why the double deception, Nellie accused of killing Judge Counsil and Bonnie's sister hung in her place? It made no damn sense, but there were answers, somewhere, someplace. Were they holding Nellie alive for some reason, hiding her away?

He went over the few facts that he had. First, Nellie hadn't killed Judge Counsil. That he'd known all along. But the judge had been killed. Nellie accused and convicted of the crime and in her place, an innocent girl hung to carry out the elaborate deception. The noose was becoming more and more twisted and he'd find out the truth and see to the paying, that he vowed silently as his big fists clenched.

Suddenly he became aware that the soft, bitter sobs had ceased from the other room. He pushed himself to his feet as he heard the sound of the back door closing. "Damn," he muttered as he raced outside, slipped on the rain-soaked ground, cursed again and regained his feet. He reached the barn door just as Bonnie emerged on the horse, the big Spencer cradled in one arm. "Don't try to stop me, Fargo," she warned.

He searched her eyes, saw the wild pain inside them. "Now, just hold on," he said.

"No," she spit out, moved the horse forward. He kept his place in front of the animal and saw the barrel of the rifle was pointed directly at him.

"Listen to me." He slipped one foot forward.

"Out of my way, goddammit," Bonnie shouted. "They just used her. Took her and hung her as some kind of decoy. I'm going to kill every damn one of them."

"Not yet," Fargo said, and edged to the side. The rifle pointed at his shoulder now. She wouldn't want to shoot him, he knew, but she was near hysteria, consumed with grief and hate. She'd react without thinking, almost beyond control of herself now. She'd also get herself killed, he realized silently. "Not yet, not till I find out more. It's not time yet," he said. He searched her eyes. They stared at him but they were far away in another world. She heard but she wasn't listening. He slid a foot out, closer, and he was to one side of the rifle barrel now. He dug heels into the wet ground, made certain he wouldn't slip and leaped forward, closed one big hand around the barrel of the rifle as he yanked. The gun blasted off, the shot sailing past his shoulder. Bonnie, still clinging to the Spencer, came out of the saddle with the gun and he caught her.

He was ready for her to fight but she only leaned hard against him and he felt her shuddered sobs. He took her back into the house, let her take off her wet clothes as he stabled the horse. She was in the short, blue nightdress when he returned, sitting on the bed, the pain still in her eyes. He pulled his wet shirt and trousers off and took her into his arms.

"They'll pay," he told her.

"Promise?" she said.

"For damn sure," he said, and the grimness was in his voice. "For damn sure."

4

Fargo draped the Ovaro's reins over the hitching post near the end of town, diagonally across from the undertaker's place. He'd spent the morning with Bonnie, talked out his thoughts with her and she felt better for it. "Maybe Nellie still has a chance," he convinced her. "I've got to find out. Going after them now might close that door."

She'd nodded understanding, her face composed, the bitter grief turned into an ache inside. "How are you going to find out?" she questioned.

"There are more than one involved in whatever it is. There'll be a weak link. There always is," he had told her, and had stayed with the thought as he rode to town. The sheriff wouldn't be it, he thought as he rode. The man backed away from trouble, but that was experience and wiliness more than weakness. He'd been around long enough to know when to back up. He was too much the old fox to be the weak link. Evans, the banker, slid across his mind next. Evans was pompous, arrogant, full of bluster, perhaps all of it hiding the hollowness inside. He'd be a good choice for a weak link if he weren't involved so deeply. Involvement would keep him strong, self-protection a kind of armor. Much the same went for Tim Smith, the mayor, Fargo knew. A nervous, insecure figure, Smith nonetheless had been able to become mayor, and in a town such as Brushville that took a shrewd eye and knowing how to do the right thing at the right time. All of that added up to its own kind of wily, cagey strength, plus his involvement.

One figure remained, Joe Holder, the undertaker with the nervous, blinking eyes. He'd been one of the two men Bonnie had seen take Carrie away the last time she was seen alive. Holder could simply have been delivering her, Fargo considered, discarded the thought. Holder was perhaps not a major figure but he was more than a delivery boy. Involved, yet not one of the inside trio, the weak link for now. Fargo turned off his thoughts, his decision and method settled in his mind. No subtle approach, no sliding around. Fear, stark naked fear. Fargo reached the undertaker's office, paused to take in the stack of four pine caskets piled atop each other outside the narrow building.

"Business seems good," he commented as he entered the office, and Joe Holder looked balefully up at him from behind the battered table.

"Some kind of shoot-out up in the hills last night," the undertaker said. "What do you want here, Fargo? You come about Nellie Noonan again, I can't help you."

"You can help yourself," Fargo said quietly. "I'm going to do you a favor." Joe Holder blinked questioningly. "I'm going to give you a chance to stay out of one of your pine boxes." Fargo watched the man blink three times in quick succession. "Where's Nellie Noonan?" he asked.

"Hung and buried," Holder said as he swallowed hard.

"Where's Carrie Akins?" Fargo questioned.

"How the hell do I know?" Holder bristled.

"You took her from her house. Nobody's seen her since," Fargo said.

"I never took her anyplace. You've been listening to that crazy sister of hers. She didn't see me. She made a mistake."

"You're getting closer to one of your boxes, Holder."

"You don't scare me, Fargo," the man said as the beads of perspiration stood out on his forehead.

"Good. I don't figure to scare you. I figure to kill you unless you start talking." Fargo spoke calmly but the steel in his voice was unmistakable. He slid from the edge of the table. "I'll be back tonight. You be here and ready to talk or you'll be wearing a wooden overcoat." He spun in his heel and strode from the office as the fear made Holder's lips tremble. Fargo saw the man pull open the drawer in the table, pull out a bottle of gin as he closed the door behind him. The next step was to lay back and watch and Fargo had just taken the reins from the hitching post when the voice called to him.

"Mister Fargo," it said, and he turned to see the woman standing beside a stylish, black-and-red cut-under buggy. Tall, she wore a black dress and a small, black bonnet from under which dark blond hair peeked. Not over thirty years old, he guessed as he took in a face that was more than attractive, almost aristocratic, a little thin, cheeks perhaps a little hollowed, yet very striking with a thin, finely shaped nose and graceful lips. Her eyes held him, pale tan irises, made to look paler by the black pupils, eyes that suggested a baked wheat field shining with a retained warmth. Her figure fit her face, long, slightly thin, yet under the black dress, swelling, well-curved breasts that seemed to struggle against demureness. "I'd like to talk to you. I'm Mariel Counsil," she said.

Fargo felt the astonishment slam into him as though it were a physical blow and knew the frown dug into his forehead. "Mariel Counsil?" he echoed.

She nodded, her pale tan eyes steady. "Judge Counsil's widow," she said.

"I'll be damned," Fargo muttered through tight lips. "Nobody told me there was a widow."

Almost the flicker of a wry smile touched her gracefully curved lips. "Would it have made any difference in the things you've been saying?" she asked.

He paused a moment. "No, it wouldn't have," he conceded. "But I'd sure as hell like to have known."

"Well, now you know," Mariel Counsil said. "I'd still like to talk with you."

"Talk," Fargo said.

"Not here," she answered. "Where we can be alone. Could you come to my place this evening, about eight?"

"Why not?" He still felt the surprise digging at him.

"Head north from town, a narrow road that curves to the left. Follow it about two miles. You'll come to a white house with green shutters. I'll be waiting there." Mariel Counsil turned and stepped into the cut-under buggy, revealed a flash of a long, slender calf. He watched her as she drove away, square shoulders back, her somewhat thin form held with its own aloofness.

"Goddamn," he muttered again as he climbed onto the Ovaro. He took the horse between two buildings, back of the one and stayed in the saddle, peering through a space that let him look out onto the street. Joe Holder's hurrying form appeared not more than a few minutes later, legs striding purposefully. Fargo moved the horse forward to where he could watch the man's progress and saw him hurry into the bank. Fargo's lips pursed in thought. Holder had hurried to the banker. Because Charley Evans was the key figure or because he was a clearing house? Either way, he'd hurried there to report, ask for instructions and protection. Fear held Joe Holder tight now and that was the important thing. Fargo moved the Ovaro out onto the main street, sat tall in the saddle as Holder came out of the bank. He saw the man's jaw drop as he spotted the Ovaro, the fear almost become panic in his face as he hurried past, eyes down. Whatever Evans had told him, it hadn't taken the fear from him and Fargo smiled in satisfaction. He ambled the Ovaro down the street, almost at the heels of the hurrying figure, sent the horse into a trot and drew up alongside the man.

"Nobody going to help you but yourself, Holder," he said as he trotted beside the man. The undertaker's face was pale as he looked up at the horseman beside him with the face of chiseled stone. "Nobody," Fargo repeated, and went the pinto into a canter, left the man behind. He allowed a wry smile to touch his lips. He didn't need to have been there to know what Charley Evans had told the undertaker. First, that Fargo was bluffing, that he was on a fishing expedition and that he knew nothing. Second, that they'd protect him. Or perhaps the banker had given him some special instructions. No matter, the banker's reassurances had been only words and words were no match for fear. Fear corroded, destroyed, ate away at a man's strength, especially when there was little strength to begin with. Joe Holder would sweat, worry and be consumed by the fear that had taken root inside him. He'd crack, decide to talk or do some fool thing. Fargo made a silent wager on it.

He reached the field and turned the Ovaro across it and the frown returned to his brow at once as he neared the house. Bonnie looked up from a washboard as he rode to a halt, swung from the saddle. "Did you know there was a Widow Counsil?" he flung at her. "Did you know the judge had a wife?"

Bonnie's face grew cautious. "Mariel Counsil? Yes, I knew it."

"Why the hell didn't you tell me that?" he roared. "I can understand the others but why didn't you tell me?"

Her face set, the stubbornness setting into her plump cheeks. "Didn't think it mattered."

"Dammit, everything matters. Maybe I'd have tried another approach if I'd known," Fargo returned.

Bonnie's face stayed stubborn and she didn't meet Fargo's eyes. "How'd you find out about her?"

"Met her. She stopped me in town. She wants to talk to me," he told her.

"You going to see her?" Bonnie still looked away.

"Damn right. Maybe she knows something. Maybe she knows it without realizing it. I've seen all the others. Why not her?" Fargo answered.

"She'll smooth-talk you, that one." Bonnie sniffed.

"How do you know so much about Mariel Counsil?"

"I knew her when she was Mariel Burton, back in Trapperstown," Bonnie said. "So did Carrie."

Fargo frowned at Bonnie's sullenness. "That's why you didn't mention her. You were afraid she'd get to me," he said, and Bonnie's silence was its own answer.

"She could always get anybody or anything she wanted," Bonnie grumbled.

"A little old-fashioned jealousy there?" Fargo prodded, and Bonnie tossed him a glare that was admission of itself. "You think she's involved?"

"I don't know. She's not going to tell you," Bonnie slid out sarcastically.

"Leave that to me," Fargo snapped, and she turned, strode into the house. "You scout the cemetery as I told you to do?" he asked, following.

She nodded. "They're still standing guard."

"Good," he grunted. "I'll be back when I get back. You stay out of trouble. Understood?"

She nodded with her face still set. He took some coffee, drank it slowly, ate some dried beef and prepared to go as the evening turned gray. He was at the door when she rushed to him, her arms around his neck, her lips hard on his. "Be careful," she said.

"Always." He grinned, patted her plump little rear and hurried to the Ovaro. He rode back toward Brushville, turned north from the end of the town and found the narrow road. It was almost dark when he came into sight of the large house, white, as she'd described, with two columns in front to give the flavor of an old southern mansion. But the rest of the house was heavy, without the grace and delicacy needed to carry through the effect of the columns. He dismounted and Mariel Counsil opened the door as he reached the columns. She seemed taller in a floor-length, dark maroon dress. A long slit on one side revealed a beautifully curved, smooth leg as she moved.

He started toward the door when he thought a tree moved at one side of the porch, frowned, and the tree moved again, became a man. Fargo looked up at a figure that never seemed to end, clothed in a black shirt and black trousers. He guessed the man to be close to seven feet, a long, gaunt face that went with his body, black hair and black coal eyes, a heavy jaw and arms that almost reached the knees that were as high as some men were tall.

"It's all right, Treeman," Mariel Counsil said. "I'm expecting this gentleman."

The long figure moved back, faded into the gathering darkness. "Treeman is a kind of personal bodyguard," Mariel Counsil said.

"Well named," Fargo commented.

"The judge got him for me some years ago," Mariel Counsil said as Fargo followed her into the house. The long dress made her seem to glide rather than take steps. "Drink?" she asked.

"Bourbon." He took in a well-furnished room of leather and wood with a large, fabric-covered settee, the walls hung with plaques and awards given to the judge. Mariel brought him the bourbon, gestured to the settee and sat down beside him, a glass of gin and lime in her hand. The slit in the dress fell open and he saw a lovely, round knee. The pale tan eyes seemed to glow, a contrast to the coolness of her slightly thin, aristocratic face.

"Thank you for coming, Fargo," she said.

"I came to listen," he answered.

"I've been very concerned about the things you've been saying, for my own reasons," Mariel Counsil said.

"Who told you about them?"

She half-smiled. "News travels fast. Some of my hands heard and told me." She took a sip of her gin and lime.

"What are your reasons?"

"You seem so certain Nellie Noonan didn't shoot the Judge."

"That's right. That what's bothering you?"

"Yes, frankly. The idea of an innocent young woman being hung is very upsetting to me. I know the others all say you're crazy, but a man that sure of himself must have reason. And now that I've met you I'm even more convinced you're not crazy."

"Thanks," he said drily.

"If there's been an injustice, I want to do something about it," Mariel Counsil said, and Bonnie's words ticked inside him. Was the woman smooth-talking him or was she being sincere? She was smart enough and attractive enough for either.

"Prove it," he snapped.

"How?" she shot back.

"Tell me what you know," Fargo said.

"Nothing much more than anyone else about the killing. I wasn't there. I was told about it by Tim Smith," Mariel Counsil said.

"The affair with Nellie Noonan, you knew about it?" Fargo questioned, his eyes hard on her, watching her every reaction.

She thought for a moment. "No, I didn't. The judge was very fond of her, I knew that. I thought it more of a father-daughter relationship. He kept referring to her as the daughter he never had."

"What are you saying?" Fargo pressed.

"I'm saying I don't think they were having an affair."

Fargo felt the surprise stab at him again. "You saying somebody made that up?"

She shrugged. "Maybe, or perhaps they had the wrong idea. But I don't believe it."

"Any other reasons?"

She hesitated again. "Yes, personal ones."

"I'd like knowing them."

"Not now. Not yet." She leaned forward and her hand touched his, stayed there and the neckline of the dress dipped enough for him to see the long swell of one white mound. "If you know anything I should know, tell me. I'll help you if I can." Her pale tan eyes were round and full of sincerity. "I don't want to be a part of something terrible, a miscarriage of justice."

He peered at Mariel Counsil, at the pale tan eyes that gazed steadily back at him. He found himself deciding that Mariel Counsil had been taken in, as much a victim of the elaborate deception as anyone. But she was still holding back, understandably, and he wondered how much he should reveal to her. Nothing yet, he decided. He'd let her prove herself a little more, first.

"Tell me about you and the judge. It seemed he liked his women a lot younger than he was," Fargo said.

"I married him because he seemed a way to what I wanted: money, power, a solid place in the community. It didn't all work out the way I thought it would."

"What are you holding back?" he pressed.

She took a long pull of the gin and lime. "I can't, not now. Let me think on it. Can you come back tomorrow night? Maybe I can find a way."

"Why not?" he answered.

She drew her hand back and her eyes lifted, studied him. "Nellie Noonan was someone special to you?"

"Not the way you mean. But she was special and she didn't kill anybody," Fargo said.

"I believe you," Mariel Counsil said. "And that

doesn't help me understand anything else about all this."

"I'll get at the truth of it." Fargo rose.

"Let me help." She stood up with him, the long, graceful swell of her breasts suddenly filling the top of the dress.

"You keep leveling with me and it's a deal," he said.

She nodded, walked to the door with him. "I'm glad you came. I've been terribly bothered. All the talk about an affair and her getting angry because he wanted out, it just didn't fit."

"Why not?"

An almost rueful smile touched her lips. "Tomorrow night." She looked beautifully sad as she closed the door. He walked down the few steps from the columns, saw movement to one side and the Colt flew into his hand as he crouched, spun. One of the trees moved, walked on long, stiff steps to the back of the house. Fargo saw the man's head almost touch the eaves of the house as he turned the corner and was out of sight. He swung onto the Ovaro and pointed the horse down the narrow road.

Mariel Counsil had been a surprise but one that was growing pleasanter. She'd done a pretty fair job of proving herself, her words coming free and openly. She was plainly suspicious that something was wrong and hadn't hesitated to admit it, just as she'd said she didn't believe there'd been an affair. His coming to town and his probing, prying accusations had obviously given substance to her own suspicions. Mariel Counsil could turn out to be not only a surprise but an ally.

He put aside further thoughts as he rode into Brushville. Night had taken most of the town to rest.

The saloon was a distant glow of light and sound as he halted at the end of town. The undertaker's building was dark downstairs but light came from a single window on the second floor. Fargo dismounted, the big Colt in his hand. It was time to find out if Holder had given in to fear or friends. Fargo began to circle the narrow building on short, careful steps, his eyes scanning the area. He tried the two doors at the rear and found them locked. There was nothing in the adjoining yard but the black, converted butcher's wagon and he returned to the front of the building, closed his hand around the doorknob and slowly pressed. The door came open and he slipped into the front room. Too small and too bare for anyone to hide in it, he crossed to the room beyond where the stacked caskets could hide the living as well as the dead.

A trickle of light filtered down the stairs as he dropped to one knee in the doorway, listened, waited, his wild-creature ears straining, listening for the faintest sound, the scrape of a shoe, the rasp of shallow breathing, a creak, a squeak, anything. But there was only the silence of the dead and he finally rose, pulled the door closed and started up the stairs. He neared the top of the stairs, the light growing bright. "Holder, you up there?" he called out, and received no reply. He halted at the top step, saw the yellow lamplight streaming from a room with a bed partly visible through the open door. He moved forward, his finger on the trigger of the big Colt, reached the doorway and peered around the doorframe into the room.

"Shit," he swore. Joe Holder was there waiting. He was also swinging from the end of a rope attached to a beam in the ceiling, his eyes no longer blinking but bulging almost out of their sockets. Fargo swore again as he used the throwing knife to sever the rope and Joe Holder's body crumpled onto the bed. Fargo saw the blood coursing through a vein in the man's temple. He stared, realization sweeping over him. Bodily functions still operated. It had to have just been done. His head lifted, his hand on the Colt, as he heard the sound from outside the single window. He raced to it, stuck his head out and saw the two figures as they dropped from the corner of the sloping roof to a small, first-floor roof landing and then to the ground. He raised the gun, pulled it down. He wanted answers and he saw the two figures streaking for the trees. They had horses hidden away there, obviously. Fargo swore again as he spun, raced down the stairs, leaping three at a time, barreled out of the building and vaulted onto the Ovaro. He spun the horse around, cut through the yard; the sound of the two fleeing horses was clear in the night. He picked up the trail at once and glimpsed the two horses cutting up through semi-open land.

He hunkered down in the saddle, sent the Ovaro full-out and the powerful horse closed distance fast. One of the fleeing riders saw him coming, fired two shots that were far off the mark. Fargo kept the pinto racing forward. He could see both men plainly now, swerving their horses in and out of small stands of black walnut. The one fired off another two shots, closer but still poor shooting. Fargo continued to keep the Ovaro closing in a straight line, eating up distance, and he saw the rider rein up to get a better shot. He touched the Ovaro lightly with one knee and the horse veered a few inches to the right. The man's shot went far off the mark again. Fargo drew the Colt from its holster. He'd have to get rid of one. Even a bad shot could get lucky.

He rose partway in the saddle, drew aim, waited for that split second between the horse's pounding forefeet and fired. The figure rose in the saddle, twisted, toppled sideways as his horse kept running. Fargo saw the second rider look back, whip his horse with his reins, try to veer up a steep incline. Fargo drew his lariat, raced the pinto to the foot of the incline. He tossed the rope, saw it whirl through the air, come down around its mark and he reined the Ovaro to a halt, took a turn around the saddle horn with the lariat and the man flew backward from his horse. Fargo saw him hit the ground, lie still and he sent the Ovaro up the incline, leaped from the saddle with the lariat in one hand, the Colt in the other. But the figure stayed motionless and Fargo stepped closer, saw the fast-spreading dark stain that ran from the back of his head where it was split open. Beneath it, he saw the sharp edge of the rock jutting up from the steep incline.

"Goddamn," he swore and cursed his luck. He'd be getting no answers this night. He reeled in his lariat and returned to the pinto, turned the horse and rode away. Mariel Counsil had been the only redeeming item for this night, he thought as he sent the horse heading for Bonnie's house.

Bonnie's eyes were sharp, probing his face when he came inside, her plump cheeks in a pout. She wore the short nightdress, sat with her legs curled up under her. "She smooth-talk you?" Bonnie tossed at him as he undid his gun belt.

"No," he told her. "Mariel Counsil isn't what you seem to think." Bonnie made a disdainful sound. "She doesn't believe Nellie had an affair with the judge." He enjoyed seeing surprise flood her face. He sat down, told her everything that Mariel had said, the frankness of her admissions. Bonnie's face stayed set when he finished but he saw her digesting his words, a tiny furrow of uncertainty touching her brow. "She smelled something wrong herself. I think she's as interested in the truth as we are."

"Still don't trust her." Bonnie sniffed.

"I think you're letting the wrong feelings get in the way of your judgment," he said, and Bonnie's face showed she didn't accept his words.

"What about Holder?" she asked.

He made a face. "Went sour. They made sure he wouldn't talk," Fargo said as he told her of finding the man. "He'd have cracked. The fear was inside him and they knew it."

"Which doesn't tell us anything."

"It tells us that he was more than an outsider. He was involved and that might mean something, soon as we find out more."

"How?" she asked with sudden despondency.

"Watch them like a hawk watches a prairie chicken. If they have Nellie someplace, they'll be going there sooner or later," he said.

"We can't watch all of them," Bonnie protested.

"We'll start with one. And maybe it's time to really make them sweat. Let me sleep on it. Maybe Mariel Counsil can help."

He saw Bonnie's face set at once, a flash of disapproval in her eyes. He undressed, lay down on the bed and turned the lamp out. He felt her push herself up beside him, her lips moving along his face, finding his mouth. "Make love to me, Fargo," she said. "Maybe that's the only good thing that'll come out of all this." He felt her legs slide along his body and his hand touched her dark warmth. Maybe she was right, he considered as he followed her wish.

He woke first with the new day, went to the well and washed and brought the bucket back for Bonnie, enjoyed the beauty of her nakedness as she bathed. She made coffee when she finished and he'd just dressed, drained the last of the bracing brew when he heard the horses come up outside. He strapped on his gun belt as Bonnie peered out the window. "Sheriff Coleman and four men," she said.

Fargo stepped outside and Bonnie went with him before he could stop her. The sheriff stayed on his horse and Fargo saw he had pinned tin deputy's badges on the four men. He also noted the four had their hands on their guns. He returned his eyes to the sheriff. "Want something?" he asked.

"I want you to drop that gun belt, first," the sheriff said.

Fargo's eyes flitted across the four men again; the sheriff now had one hand on his gun too. He could get two, three, but not five. Hot lead would spray in all directions. Bonnie would surely take more than one bullet. He unbuckled the gun belt, let it slide down his legs to the ground. "What the hell is all this about?" he growled at the sheriff.

The man's beefy face managed to take on a crude smugness. "I'm arresting you, Fargo."

"Hell, you know you can't arrest anyone for asking questions," Fargo said. "What kind of shit is this?"

The sheriff smiled. "I'm arresting you for killing Joe Holder."

Fargo felt the words fly to his lips, pulled them

back. Putting himself at the scene would only make it worse. "I didn't kill him. Is he dead?"

"You know goddamn well he's dead," Sheriff Coleman barked. "You killed him."

"Somebody else," Fargo said.

"You threatened him. You said you'd put him in one of his pine boxes," the sheriff said. "He told Charley Evans. Abe Altdorf, the bank teller, heard him say it. You threatened him and you did it. You're under arrest for murder, Fargo. Get your horse."

"This is a stinking frame-up," Bonnie cut in, and Fargo silenced her with a sharp glance, returned his eyes to the sheriff. He'd underestimated the man. The sheriff had seen his chance and seized it. Fargo started for the barn to get the Ovaro and two of the sheriff's brand-new deputies went with him, one scooping up his gun belt. Bonnie came to stand beside him as he saddled the Ovaro, her whisper fierce. "You going to let them do this? They'll hang you fast."

"Not much I can do about it now without getting us both killed," he said. "Stay back, stick to the house, stay cool. Don't count me out too fast." He climbed onto the Ovaro and wished he felt as confident as he'd let on with Bonnie. Her brown eyes were full of troubled concern as she watched him ride off with the sheriff and the other four men.

"How'd you know I was here?" he asked Sheriff Coleman as they rode across the field.

"You seemed chummy with the Akins girl. I figured you might be holed up with her," the sheriff said. The rest of the ride to Brushville was in silence and Fargo saw that the sheriff had his four deputies ride with their guns drawn. A backhanded compliment, he smiled wryly, but it left him with no chance for a break. Reaching town, the sheriff had him put into the first cell where everyone in the front office could keep an eye on him. Fargo sat down on the stone bench in the cell. Time was no ally but it was all he had for the moment. He'd wait for the night watch, he decided, and closed his eyes, dozed as the day wore on. Frustration drained the system. Waiting was a learned skill and one he had long mastered. He stretched out, let himself doze, relax, as he turned possibilities for a break in his mind in unhurried fashion.

It was midafternoon when the sheriff paused at the cell. "You know you're done for, Fargo," the man said.

Fargo met his cold gaze. "I don't know about me but I know about you," he returned.

The man's face broke into a snarl. "You're a hard-nosed bastard, aren't you?" he barked as he stalked back to his office. Fargo closed his eyes, let himself doze again on the stone bench. The day was nearing an end when the voices woke him, one a woman's voice from the outer office. He swung from the bench, went to the cell door and felt the astonishment dig into him as he saw Mariel Counsil there with the sheriff.

"You heard right. We've got him here for killing Joe Holder," Fargo heard the sheriff say.

"He didn't do it," he heard Mariel answer and the astonishment wrapped itself around him.

"Now, meaning no disrespect, Mrs. Counsil, but how the hell do you know that?" the sheriff returned.

Fargo saw Mariel's pale tan eyes look at the sheriff with cool, contained calmness. "Because he spent the night with me," she said. Fargo watched the sheriff as he stared at the young woman.

"Goddamn, Mrs. Counsil, you don't want to say that," the man blurted out.

"But I am saying it. Let him go. He didn't do it," Mariel ordered.

"You say that and I let him go, it'll have to go on record, ma'am," the sheriff told her. "I'm not the only one who sees the records."

"I understand," Mariel said calmly. "He was with me last night. You've no cause to hold him now."

"Yes, ma'am," the sheriff said, and Fargo straightened as the man walked to the cell, took the cell keys from his pocket, his face dark and full of anger. "You're one goddamn lucky man, Fargo," he muttered.

"And you're one lying bastard," Fargo answered as he walked from the cell. Mariel's pale tan eyes met his and she said nothing as the sheriff handed him his gun belt back. He walked from the office with her, saw she had a light-boned chestnut waiting. A man brought the Ovaro to him and he swung into the saddle, rode in silence beside her in the gathering darkness until they were outside of town.

"I owe you," he said. "What made you do it?" His eyes stayed on her, saw her lips form a beautiful, almost sad smile.

"Different things," she said.

"Name some," he said.

"I didn't finish telling you things last night. Couldn't do it with you in a jail cell," Mariel Counsil said.

"Next one," Fargo said.

"You said I had to prove myself." Her eyes met his gaze.

"You did," he grunted. "And then some." He tossed the question at her as he probed her eyes. "How do you know I didn't kill Holder?"

"I don't," she answered. "But I'd wager you didn't. I heard he'd been hung. That wouldn't be your style, in the first place."

"And in the second place?"

"You wouldn't have wanted him dead. You wanted him to crack, to talk. He couldn't do that dead," Mariel answered.

"You think things out real good," Fargo commented as they reached her house. The tall figure seemed almost one of the columns alongside it as Fargo dismounted, helped Mariel from her horse. Fargo felt the huge man's deep eyes on him as he went into the house, closed the door behind him. "Why don't I think he likes me?" Fargo asked.

"Treeman doesn't like anyone." She opened a wooden cabinet. "I need a drink." She poured bourbon for him and gin and lime for herself. She sat down beside him and he saw she wore a tan blouse over her riding skirt, the top buttons undone and the slow, long curve of her breasts pressed against the material. She downed her drink quickly and he finished the bourbon, met her pale tan eyes as she looked up at him. "The judge having an affair with Nellie Noonan, you wanted to know why it didn't fit," she said.

"That's right." He nodded.

She leaned forward and her mouth came over his as she put the glass down. He felt her tongue darting out instantly, flicking over his lips and her hands were digging into his shoulders. The act and the intensity took him aback. "I'll show you," Mariel Counsil breathed. "I'll show you." He felt her hand slip from his shoulders, tear at the buttons of his shirt as her tongue continued to push into his mouth, quick, thrusting little motions. She paused, her hands

104

going to her blouse and he heard two buttons tear away as she ripped the garment open. "Oh, Christ," she gasped, and drew back for an instant, enough time for him to take in the long curve of her breasts, hanging down to lift at the undersides with sudden fullness, nipples hard and brown pink, almost as large as the very tiny areolas that surrounded each. Her hands rose, clasped his face between them and her mouth opened, gasped, her tongue flicking out into the air, pleading, searching. She pulled his mouth down to it, pushed the soft wet little organ deep into his mouth. "Fuck me," he heard Mariel Counsil breathe. "Fuck me, Fargo, now, now, now . . . oh, Jesus, fuck me."

She half rose, pushed the riding skirt down, tore away black bloomers and Fargo pulled off clothes, fell onto the rug with her as she seemed frenzied, her mouth working feverishly, her white cream abdomen sucking in and out of its own. He grasped her shoulders, pressed her back and held her in place. "Mariel . . . easy," he said. "Easy." She shook her head, tried to push away from his grip.

"No, no, don't hold me, don't stop me," she cried out. But he held his grip on her, watched her long-hipped figure writhe, smooth whiteness with an appropriately long, narrow curly bush, aristocratic in its own way. The word kept coming to his mind and he grew annoyed. It was wrong. Mariel's face had all the surface planes of aristocracy and yet it missed, cheeks a trifle too hollow, pale tan, smoldering eyes that didn't match her body. And now the frenzy of her, all earth and fire, almost savage. As if an answer to his thoughts, she raised one leg, kicked at him and he released her shoulders. She flew at him instantly, long rib cage rubbing against his body, long legs twisting to wrap around him. He was ready and eager, her wildness arousing of itself. He pushed into her and it was almost as though he had entered a vial of warm fluid.

"Yes, now, fuck me ... Jesus Christ, Fargo, help me, help me," she screamed in his ear. He thrust harder, deeper, began to pump furiously and she screamed out the words in ecstasy, pumping with him; her long breasts fell from side to side as her torso twisted and writhed as she urged the body to explode, tear at itself, encompass all ecstasy at once. He felt her belly, surprisingly round for the rest of her body, ram up hard against his abdomen. Her scream began as a sound pulled from deep inside her, became frenzied words. "Yes, oh, oh ... I'm coming, coming ... Iiiiiiieee ... ah, Jesus Christ ... fuck ... oh, fuck ... iiiiieeee," and suddenly she was clinging to him completely, attached to him, hanging on to him with legs, arms, suctioned flesh and the moment seemed suspended in nothingness, unable to absorb the pure physical power of its existence. Then, with something that sounded not unlike a puma's angry snarl, she flung herself away from him, landed on her back to lie there with her arms and legs spread-eagled, the long, lovely torso quivering, her legs twitching.

"Jesus," Mariel Counsil breathed. "Jesus that was good, oh, so good." Fargo moved to her, rested on his abdomen and his arms as she sat up suddenly, a tiny fold of flesh creasing the top of her round belly. Her eyes stared at him and he saw the anger in their tan paleness. "Did that answer you?" she demanded angrily. "He hadn't given it to me in five years. He couldn't. I found that out on our first night married. He tried for a while but it was no go and finally he even stopped trying. That's how I knew there was no affair with Nellie Noonan, not with her, not with anybody." Fargo nodded and her anger turned aside any attempt at sympathy. "And I couldn't get it elsewhere, not the judge's wife, oh, no. He had me watched day and night for five years, day and night."

"Till now," Fargo said.

"Till now," she echoed, a hiss in her voice and she turned, came against him. Her hand reached down, moved along his steel-spring thighs. "Not just once tonight, not after all this time," she breathed. "Jesus, no, Fargo." Her hands grasped at him and she was almost frenzied again as she rubbed against him, bent down with both hands to cradle his organ as it instantly grew, answered, her frenzied wanting its own contagion. Mariel Counsil swung her legs over him, came onto him, pushed herself onto his erectness, rammed herself down as hard as she could. "Iiiieee ... iiiiee ... yes, yes ... oh, my God, I want it, I want it, I want it," she screamed. With each ramming thrust of her onto him she screamed the words, fell forward, pushed one long breast into his mouth almost with savage glee. "Take it, take it ... take it," she cried out as he half swallowed the soft mound, the brown-pink nipple hard against his tongue.

Her narrow, flat curly triangle pressed onto his pelvis and he suddenly felt the quivering begin, the contractions tighten around his own throbbing. She bore down harder, soft, wet lips flattening against him, her wanting flowing out onto him. Mariel lifted her head, reared back, her long breasts shaking, and she drew her legs up under her, as though she were in the saddle and began to leap up and down on him, screaming with each leap. With a violent suddenness, her legs straightened, shot out forward as she leaned her body back, supported herself with the palms of her hands pressed flat on the rug. She throbbed over him and her little rounded belly shook violently. The gargled scream came from her with the last shuddered contraction, the sound wrapped in the eternal moment, only to die away with a whispered groan. "More . . . oh, more . . . Jesus," Mariel Counsil protested as she fell backward, rolled from him to lie panting hard at his side.

He pushed himself onto his elbows, found himself staring at her. It had been no less frenzied, no less wild the second time. Perhaps not all made of pent-up desire, he pondered. There was a savagery, a frantic fury to her lovemaking that seemed to go beyond pent-up wanting. He watched her as her panting grew less and she finally sat up, leaned back and let him enjoy the sight of her long, supple body. "Enough proving? Enough showing why?" she asked, and he nodded. It had been more than enough, no deception in her passion, her wanting too encompassing to be anything but real. "I still don't understand any of it," Mariel Counsil said. "Why did they make up that story of an affair? Do you know?"

"Some of it." He nodded. "They killed the judge and they needed a killer, a scapegoat. That's where they made their mistake. They picked the wrong scapegoat."

"Why do you say that?" He sat back, told her about Nellie and when he finished she stared at him, digesting his words. A small, strangely rueful smile came to touch her lips, finally. "They'd no way of knowing that, of course," she said. "A twist of fate."

"There's more," he said. "They didn't hang Nellie Noonan. They hung somebody else in her place."

Mariel Counsil stared at him and he saw the astonishment flood her face. "How do you know that?" she questioned.

He hesitated, decided to hold back. Knowing too much could put her in danger. "I know."

"You're guessing that because they refused to let you see Nellie in the box," Mariel said.

He shrugged. "Whatever," he said. "I'm sure enough."

She continued to stare at him, frowning, her eyes trying to see behind his words. "Which means what?"

"They're holding Nellie someplace, for some reason, if they haven't done with her by now," he said. "You can help me find out."

"How?" she asked quickly.

"I want my hands on Charley Evans. Get him out here. You can easily find an excuse."

"Yes, I suppose I could." She frowned in thought.

"Will you do it?"

"Yes, of course. I'll set it up and be in touch," she said. He rose, pulled on clothes and she watched him, slid into the full-length dress only when he finished. "Thanks, for being understanding," she said. "I'd like to say thanks again soon."

He shrugged. "First things first. But I'll be around."

Mariel Counsil's smile was made of small triumph as she watched him from the door. He swung onto the Ovaro and paused as he glimpsed the giant figure nearby, motionless as a tree trunk. He felt the man's eyes watching him as he rode away, burning into him. Treeman was a strangely ominous figure, he decided; a quality of silent evil seemed to exude from the man. He turned the pinto down the narrow road and finally across the open meadowland.

Bonnie heard him as he rode up and he saw the light in the window go off, the muzzle of the big old

Spencer poke through the open bottom of the window. "It's me," he called. The lamp went on and the front door flew open as Bonnie stared at him.

"You break out?" She frowned.

"Not exactly." He dismounted, led the horse into the barn and returned to the house, Bonnie's eyes still questioning. "Mariel Counsil got me out," he said. Bonnie's frown dug harder into her forehead, her stare one of disbelief. "She'd heard and she came through for me. She stuck her neck out as my alibi." Fargo told her what Mariel had done to force the sheriff to let him go free.

Bonnie's frown stayed as she stared at him. "Why?" she murmured. "Why'd she do it?"

"I told you. She wants to know the truth. She wants to find out what really happened to her husband," Fargo said.

Bonnie took in his answer and he saw the wariness cling to her eyes. "Maybe." She sniffed.

"She's proved herself," Fargo said.

"By getting you out?"

"Yes. She put her reputation out to do it," he said. "And there was more."

"Such as?"

He picked phrases with care. "Other things she said, told me about, her frankness," he answered.

"I'll bet." Bonnie sniffed sullenly.

"Why are you so damned skeptical?" he tossed at her.

"I don't trust her. I think she smooth-talked you or did better," Bonnie said, and he marveled silently at the accuracy of female intuition.

"She's been honest and she's helping me. She's getting Evans there for me," he said.

Bonnie digested his words and decided against

110

further comment. He took off clothes and stretched out on the bed after turning out the lamp. Tiredness deepened his sleep. He felt Bonnie come to bed and keep distant, and was content to let it stay that way. When he woke in the morning she was curled up like a little ball on the other side of the bed. He rose, washed and dressed, took the Ovaro and made a scouting trip to the cemetery. The two guards were still there and he turned back to the house. Bonnie was up when he arrived and had coffee and breakfast cakes on.

"What happens, now?" she asked him.

"I wait for word from Mariel," he said. "I won't take the chance of losing Evans the way I did Holder."

"Maybe he won't tell you anything."

"I'll convince otherwise," Fargo said tightly. He used the rest of the morning to clean and oil the Colt and the Sharps. It was a little past midday when the horseman appeared, moving slowly across the field toward the house. Fargo went outside and watched the giant of a figure astride the horse. The man rode a big, heavy draft horse, mostly Percheron, with thick legs, a wide, strong back and magnificently muscled chest. Even so, Treeman's legs almost reached the ground. The man's black coal eyes stared malevolently as he handed over a small envelope. Fargo tore it open, read the few lines on the notepaper inside:

He's coming here tonight. Eight o'clock.

M.

He folded the note, looked up to see that Treeman had already turned the huge horse around and was riding slowly away. The giant figure's ominousness remained in daylight as well as dark, Fargo noted.

He turned and Bonnie waited inside as he entered. "It's set up for tonight," he told her.

"I'll go with you," she said.

"No. I don't know what I'll run into. Maybe he won't come alone. I don't want to be worrying about you."

"I'll take care of myself." She glowered back at him.

His eyes fastened her. "You want to be in on the finish? Then don't get in the way now." His words, promise and admonishment, hit home and she turned away, not happy but grudging acceptance in her face. "I won't cut you out," he said gently, and she nodded, the glower fading.

The remainder of the day passed quickly and he was in the saddle as dusk crept across the land, headed for Mariel Counsil. "Be careful," Bonnie had said, kissed him with the sweetness that was half of her, as he'd left. He rode the narrow path at a canter. Dark had just swallowed up the day as he reached the white, columned house. He spotted the giant, omnipresent figure to one side, amid the trees, motionless, watching.

Mariel opened the door a slit and Fargo slipped into the house. She wore the full-length maroon dress and he saw the half-finished gin and lime on the table as she led him into a bedroom that adjoined the living room. "Wait in here. I'll stay in the other room. I want everything to look normal," she said.

"Nervous?" he asked.

She hesitated before answering. "Excited," she replied. She hurried into the living room and left the door open a crack but it was more than enough for him to fully view the other room. He watched her sit

112

down, sip on her drink and tenseness drew her slightly hollow cheeks in deeper. Somehow, it didn't take away from her attractiveness. Fargo moved to the bed, stretched out on it, hands behind his back and he lay still and listened to the silence. A small frown touched him after almost an hour had passed. Evans was late. The minutes continued to tick away, became another half hour and the banker continued to be late. Fargo rose, went to the door and peered through the crack. Mariel stood near the window, peering out, arms folded just under her breasts. He went back and stretched out on the bed again. He let another half hour go by and felt the uneasiness growing inside him, forced himself to stay for fifteen minutes more then pushed himself to his feet, a grimness settling inside him. He pushed the door open and Muriel rose from the settee, her eyes wide, helpless.

"Bankers are usually punctual," Fargo said.

She nodded. "He always is."

"He's not coming. Something went wrong."

"Maybe he was delayed?"

"For two hours?" Fargo grunted. "No, something's wrong."

"I don't understand it." Mariel shrugged.

"You think maybe he smelled a rat?"

"Why would he?"

"You can be sure Coleman told him you'd bailed me out, and the reason you gave. Maybe he figured we were too chummy suddenly and decided to back off," Fargo ventured.

She shrugged. "I suppose it is possible."

Fargo nodded agreement. It was more than possible and he felt the uneasiness on him as he started for the door. Her hand pulled at his arm. "No, don't go," she said.

"I'd best. I feel edgy. But thanks for trying."

Her hand stayed closed around his arm. "No, not yet," she said, and he saw the simmering in the pale tan eyes. "Christ, I've been burning up all day thinking about you, about last night. All those years and now you. Too much . . . I want more . . . I need it, God, I need it."

"Next time around," he said.

Her dark blond hair shook vigorously. "No, now . . . now," she breathed as she dropped to both knees. Her fingers tore at buttons, pulled his trousers open and her hand had already reached in, groping, finding him. "Oh, Christ," she panted, drew him out and tugged with both hands, pushing material aside, bringing out all of him. Fargo felt himself responding as once again her frenzied wanting was a sweeping, infectious force and he felt himself ballooning. "Oh, Jesus, yes," he heard her cry as he thickened in her hand.

"What the hell. Never refuse a lady," Fargo muttered as though the decision hadn't already been made by another part of him that responded with eager willingness. He dropped gun belt and clothes as Mariel wriggled out of her dress. He sank down on the rug with her and she buried her face between his legs and made little sounds of animal enjoyment, writhed, pulled, pushed and her frenzy was the overwhelming fire that ignited everything near it. He felt his own spiraling wanting, pulled her up, turned her over on the rug, clamped down on one lovely, long breast with less than gentleness.

"Oh, God . . . oh . . . yes, Jesus, yes . . . I love it, love it," she gasped, pushed her breasts at him, demanded he take first one then the other deep into his mouth as he felt her hips lifting, pumping convulsively. He swung over onto her, thrust forward and she leaped upward to meet his organ, frantic pushing, pumping frenzy. Once more, he felt the savagery in her, the out-of-control desire that seemed to turn her into a special kind of madwoman. Her hands clawed at him, pulled and she cried out with his most furious thrusts, but only for more. When the moment erupted, there was no time standing still, no pause to savor the ultimate, not for Mariel Counsil. She pumped with frantic fury, her scream mingling with the soft slapping of flesh on flesh. "Ah! Ah! Ah!" she screamed with each pumping thrust against him, with each clap of her flesh against his pelvis. And when the terrible power vanished away with instantaneous ending, she flung herself from him to lay facedown on the floor, her fingers clawing into the rug as her body twitched and her hard panting was a protest of the body.

He rose, drew a deep breath, felt drained for a moment, her power immense. He pulled clothes on, let his own breath return. He was finished dressing when she turned, stared up at him, the pale tan eyes almost veiled. "Till next time," she said softly.

"Find out what happened to Evans," Fargo said as he left and hurried into the night. The silent giant hadn't moved an inch, he noted as he swung onto the Ovaro and rode away in a fast canter. The uneasiness wrapped itself around him again as he rode and wondered why the banker hadn't shown. If the man had indeed become suspicious about Mariel, that ended her being of practical help. It'd also make Evans more careful, he realized. But no matter, he couldn't stay back waiting any longer. He had to make something break. He was still pondering his next move as he left the narrow road, cut across the field and saw the lamp on in the window of Bonnie's house as he came in sight. He reached the house, swung from the horse, a little surprised Bonnie hadn't flung the door open with a score of questions bursting from her.

He stepped to the door, pushed it open and froze. Curses and rage spiraled inside him as he surveyed the room, chairs overturned, one smashed, an iron pot halfway across the floor, a torn piece of Bonnie's shirt on one overturned chair. And nothing more but the silence. "Sons of bitches," he swore. They'd taken her. She had put up a fierce fight but they'd taken her.

5

He cursed as he took the kerosene lamp and raced from the house to drop to one knee outside, holding the lamp up to light the ground. The prints were plain enough—five, maybe six horses, he guessed. One would be Bonnie's and his eyes followed the prints from where they had milled together to where they led off north. He lowered the lamp, put it inside the house and ran back to the Ovaro, paused to cast a glance at the sky. Not enough moonlight to follow a trail for most men. Just enough for him. He sent the Ovaro after the trail of the fleeing horsemen and saw that the trail stayed north, turned into the hill country.

They stayed at the very edge of the long stands of Douglas fir and bigcone spruce, keeping just out of the forest to let them make better time. He grunted with grim satisfaction. It also let him gain on them with no need to move slow, eyes searching the night ground. A knot of horses moving fast together bruised a wide swath of branch ends and leaves to provide a clear trail. He paused at a large cluster of young branches that had been bruised and snapped, ran the tips of his fingers over the broken ends. Still wet, fresh, he noted. They were perhaps two hours ahead, he estimated as he pushed the pinto on.

Thoughts pushed at him with the rapid-fire pounding of the Ovaro's hooves. Why had they decided to strike suddenly? And why at Bonnie? Had they come looking for him, found only Bonnie and decided to take her? Other questions crowded in. Was this the reason Evans hadn't kept his appointment with Mariel? Or had others told the banker to stay away, afraid he might spill something? Something had sent them into action, triggered the sudden strike. Something, Fargo pondered. They may have decided to try to silence him again. Taking Bonnie gave them a hostage, at least. Perhaps it had been but another attempt by Sheriff Coleman to do what he failed to do the first time. But the banker would have kept his appointment with Mariel, the two things unconnected. Or were they? Could they have suddenly grown suspicious of Mariel? The questions stabbed and twisted inside him as he raced through the night. Each was entirely possible yet none satisfied. Something unformed nagged inside him. Something. His lips pressed hard into each other and he pushed aside further speculation. They had Bonnie. That came first and he leaned forward in the saddle, concentrating all his thoughts on the pursuit.

They had stayed at the edge of the forest, following the trees that curved into the hill country. Many of the leaves, brushed inward as they passed, hadn't begun to spring back into place, he noted. He was gaining quickly on them. They had slowed, feeling safe. He went on for another fifteen minutes when he picked up the sound of the horses moving ahead of him. He slowed the pinto out of a hoof-pounding gallop to a soft trot that still gained ground and he glimpsed the small knot of horses as they crested a rise in the hill. He continued to close the distance, moving near enough to count six horses, the one carrying Bonnie kept in the center. He slowed, afraid to come any nearer. If one glanced back by chance, surprise would be gone and he needed surprise. He steered the Ovaro into the forest, held just inside the edge of the tree line where enough of the dim moonlight came in to let him make time through the thick firs. As he caught up to the horsemen he veered into the woods a little more, drew almost abreast of the riders just outside the trees.

The pounding hooves of their own horses kept them from hearing the Ovaro as he rode parallel to them and he drew the big Colt .45 from its holster. One of the riders, a chunky-bodied man with his hat worn low on his forehead, rode lead. The others flanked Bonnie, two on each side of her. Fargo raised the Colt. The nearest two of Bonnie's flankers, he decided, took aim, waited as trees and branches flickered by the horses almost as a protective curtain. But a gap appeared and he was ready, the Colt raised to fire. His two shots sounded almost as one and the two riders, as though they were part of a trick-riding exhibition, leaped up out of their saddles, twisted in unison and pitched sideways from their horses.

Fargo glimpsed Bonnie's jaw drop open in surprise and fright as she stared into the dark of the woods. The man riding lead was quickest of the remaining three to react as he swung his horse into the trees and sprang out of the saddle at once. "Hit the ground," Fargo yelled at Bonnie as he tried to level his gun at the two riders on the other side of her. She reined up, leaped to the ground, but the precious seconds were gone, the two men already diving from their mounts. The shot tore through the trees in front of him and Fargo dropped low in the saddle, heard the bullet crack into a branch just over his head. He half rolled, half dived from the Ovaro as the man fired again, landed in the underbrush and rolled, rolled again and swung himself behind a thick bigcone spruce.

"He's in here. Get the bastard," the chunky one shouted, and Fargo saw the other two darting between trees, hardly more than shadowed shapes. He held his fire.

"Stay flat," he yelled, aware all would know to whom he called. A shot slammed into the tree beside him. He saw a darting shape find shelter behind a tree, another flitting shadow race to his left. He grimaced and swore silently. He didn't like it. They were working toward him and spread out too far to take in one deadly volley. Zeroing in on one would reveal his position to the other two. He waited, gathered powerful leg muscles, drew in his breath and began to rise, streaking toward another tree. The shots erupted at once, from three separate directions.

"Aaaagh . . . agh, oh . . . ooooh," he cried out as he flung himself through a half-dozen low branches, landed in the brush, kicked his legs hard against the leaves.

"We got him," he heard the voice shout and heard the three figures start forward through the trees. But another small explosion of sound came from the nearby bushes and he saw Bonnie rise, race toward where he lay. No, he breathed inwardly, no. But Bonnie spotted him, fell to her knees beside him. *Shit*, he swore in silent frustration.

"Oh, damn, damn, Fargo," Bonnie choked out. "I'm sorry, Fargo . . . Jesus, I'm sorry." His eyes seemed closed in death but he peered up at her through tiny slits as she bent over him, her face shrouded in despair.

"Get out of the goddamn way," he whispered through lips that didn't move. He saw Bonnie's eyes pop open wide, her lips part. But it was too late as he saw the three figures come into view over her shoulder. "Stay there," he whispered fiercely. "Let them pull you away."

She was still staring at him, bent over him as the figure came up behind her. The man's hand closed over her shoulder and Fargo saw a second man come up beside him. "On your feet," he heard the man rasp at Bonnie as he pulled her up, started to swing her to one side. Bonnie screamed as the man holding her became a fountain spouting red from his chest. Before the second figure could bring his gun to bear, Fargo's next shot blew the top of his head off, as though he'd been magically scalped. Bonnie was still screaming as she fell to the ground and Fargo rolled as the chunky man fired two shots, flung his empty gun after the bullets and followed with a hurtling dive. The chunky figure landed atop Fargo as the Trailsman tried to bring his gun up, felt his arm knocked aside. The man leaped, tried to bring his both knees down on the bigger man's groin but Fargo managed to twist away, caught one knee against his hip. He swung a powerful arm backward, crashed it against the man's head and felt the thick torso fall away from him. He spun, got to one knee, the Colt still in his hand. He saw the knife appear in the man's hand and the chunky shape leaped at him, the blade held straight as though it were a short spear. Fargo swore as he saw that even if his shot slammed into the man, the momentum of the hurtling figure would plunge the blade into him. He threw himself backward and landed on the flat of his back, saw the knife and the thick body behind it hurtle over him. The man tried to stop his momentum, bring his hand down with the knife onto the figure below him but Fargo fired from his prone position as the thick body passed over him. The shot shattered the man's pelvis and his scream of anguish ended in a guttural choking sound as he dropped facedown, his legs and torso jerking with short, convulsive movements until, with a final shudder, he lay still.

Fargo pushed himself to his feet, looked around to see Bonnie slowly getting up. She stumbled to him, leaned her head against his chest, finally drew back. "Sorry about before," she said. "Damn you."

"Right sentiments, wrong timing." He grinned. "Now get your horse. We've a lot to do and not enough time to do it."

"I want to stop back at the house. This shirt's in pieces," she said as she rode beside him.

"I want to get to Evans's place," he told her.

"It's on the way," she said.

"Were they looking for me?" he asked.

Bonnie frowned in thought. "No, I don't think they were, now that you ask. They told me, 'You're going with us,' never asked about you."

Fargo's frown stayed. "They say anything else? *Anything?*"

She thought back again. "No. But there was a sixth one. He went back to tell somebody they had me. Sheriff Coleman, I figured." Fargo nodded, said nothing. "What happened with Charley Evans?" Bonnie asked.

"He never showed."

"You think they got suspicious?"

"Why would they get suspicious of Mariel? All of a sudden like that?" he mused aloud. "Something's wrong, someplace. Something's missing. Evans is going to tell me what," he said, his voice harsh.

"Tell *us*," Bonnie corrected. "I'm not sitting around waiting anymore. " He shrugged. He couldn't blame her and he'd no taste for arguing it out. She'd been part of it from the start. She deserved to be in on the finish and he had the feeling that the finish was coming faster than he'd expected. He rode in silence and the nagging thoughts continued to swirl through him. He stayed in the saddle when they reached Bonnie's house and she ran in, emerged in minutes with a dark green shirt on and the old Spencer in one hand. Fargo's eyes lifted to the sky. The hours had brought dawn near and his mouth set tight as she led the way to the banker's house on the other side of the big field of bergamot. He halted the Ovaro under a big hackberry near the house, surveyed the silent darkness of the structure.

"He's likely to sleep at this hour," Bonnie said.

"You check the barn." She frowned at him. "See if his horse is there," he said in annoyance. Bonnie dismounted, headed for the barn as he made his way to the back of the house and found the rear door. It was locked; he was putting pressure on the lock as he turned the knob slowly, trying to force it to snap open, when Bonnie came up.

"The barn's empty. No horse," she said.

"Get down," he told her as he stepped to a nearby window in the house, used the butt of the Colt to smash it open. "We'll wake him up if he's in there."

Fargo dropped down as the window shattered. He waited, listening, but there was no sound of anyone waking inside. "He's not there." Fargo took long steps to the barn door as the first gray dawn light slipped over the land. He knelt down, picked out hoofprints, followed them as they separated from others. Two horses, he thought, the prints not more than a few hours old. He got to his feet, strode to the Ovaro. "Let's move," he barked at Bonnie. He set a fast pace and saw the two horses had gone north into the hill country. They'd followed only a few minutes when Bonnie glanced at him.

"Same direction those varmints were taking me," she said, and Fargo nodded, rode for a few minutes more and reined to a halt. He pointed to a high ridge where a line of balsam firs stood etched against the gray dawn sky.

"I'll meet you up there," he said.

"Where are you going?" she asked at once.

"I'm being nagged. I've got to put a stop to it." He spurred the Ovaro off in a fast canter before she could ask further. He saw her watch him go for a few moments, then continue on. He rode hard in the new day's grayness, crossed the low hills and slowed when he finally reached the cemetery. He scanned the area, eyes narrowed. The two guards were gone and he rode in, along the perimeter of the graveyard to halt at the new site on the far edge. He peered down at the earth where he had patted it down when he'd finished his ghoulish task, stared for a long minute and then wheeled the pinto in a tight circle. A harsh sound escaped his lips as he galloped away, kept the pace as streaks of pink began to cut across the sky. He caught up to Bonnie before she reached the line of balsams, slowed, fell in beside her.

"Satisfy yourself?" she commented, the question asking more than it appeared to.

"Enough," he grunted.

"That all you're going to say?" She glared.

"For now." He halted to examine the ground. The two horses had turned to ride east along the ridge, just this side of the balsams and he followed. The morning grew into itself as the trail moved through wooded land, across the stream and up a tree-covered hillside. He put his arm out, reined up suddenly as he glimpsed the house ahead where the land grew flat but still heavily timbered. He dismounted, motioned to Bonnie and she slid from her horse, the Spencer in her hands. He moved forward and the house grew clear, a log house, no longer new, long and narrow, isinglass windows along one long side. Fargo dropped to a crouch, pulled Bonnie down beside him as Charley Evans came from the house with a bucket. The banker, in shirt-sleeves, walked to a well, pumped water as a man in a tall, tan hat emerged from the house.

"That's the one who left the others to report," Bonnie whispered. Others came out, some with tin cups, trooped to the well. He heard Bonnie's tiny gasp of surprise as Tim Smith appeared, his beefy face haggard, his eyes red-rimmed. Sheriff Coleman, fully clothed with gun belt on, was the last to come from the house. "They're all here," Bonnie breathed, and he nodded. "You're not surprised," she said.

"No," he said as he made a fast count. Evans, the mayor and Sheriff Coleman plus three hired guns.

"I'll wager a good payroll there's somebody else inside."

Her eyes peered at him. "Nellie Noonan?" He nodded. "How are you going to find out?"

"Get inside," he said, his eyes going to one of the hired hands as the man went to his horse. "They're going to do things. Some, anyway." He settled down and Bonnie pressed against him as his eyes watched the scene. The hired gun continued to see to the horses as the others returned to the house to emerge a half hour later. Fargo's eyes flicked up through the branches over his head. The sun was nearing noon. His eyes returned to the men as they paused outside the house. Coleman seemed in charge of the immediate moves.

"You and Abe go down the north ridge," the sheriff told two of the hired hands. "I'll look west with Tim." He turned to the banker. "You and Sam try south."

"This is a waste of time," the banker said. "It's not going to be anywhere around here."

"This was his place. It could be. You've nothing to do till tonight. Maybe we'll get lucky," the sheriff barked back, strode to his horse and mounted the animal. He rode off with the mayor and Fargo watched the others go off in pairs, stayed motionless until they were out of sight.

"What was that all about?" Bonnie asked as she rose with him.

"Damned if I know but they'll be coming back." Fargo strode from the trees, trotted to the door of the house, paused, listened, then pushed his way inside. A narrow front room greeted him, straight-backed wood chairs around a table, a cabinet and little else except for the fireplace. Three doorways indicated other rooms down a narrow hallway. Fargo moved on long steps past the first two, glanced in to see wooden cots and little else in each. The last room was larger, a battered bed inside it and he halted, drew in breath as Bonnie came up behind him.

"My God," he heard her breathe as his eyes held on the small, naked figure tied to the top bedposts. "My God," Bonnie repeated as he stepped into the room, approached the bed on slow, careful steps. His eyes moved up and down Nellie Noonan's slender, small-breasted form, trying to find a place that was not cut, scraped, black-and-blue, beaten, burned or smeared with dried blood. She lay with eyes closed and he leaned down, listened to the sound of her almost inaudible breathing. Her body bore a hundred ugly welts, some plainly the result of a blunt instrument, others the torn, raw ones made by a whip. Her nipples were raw marks, charred flesh burned away, her breasts scarred and crisscrossed with red, torn flesh.

"They've been torturing her," Bonnie gasped. "The bastards. The rotten, stinking beasts. Is she alive?"

"Just about," Fargo said. He bent closer to the bruised, battered face. "Nellie," he said softly. "Nellie, can you hear me. It's Fargo, Nellie . . . Fargo." He watched and saw no sign, not even the flicker of an eyelid. She lay absolutely still, only the shallow, faint breathing evidence that she lived. He heard Bonnie turn away, draw her breath in, fight off being sick.

"Why? My God, why? Jesus, maybe Carrie was better off being just hung?"

"They've been trying to get something out of her," Fargo said. "The stupid sons of bitches. The goddamn rotten morons." Bonnie stared back. "She doesn't know whatever they think she knows. She'd have told them if she did. They're too goddamn dumb to realize that."

"What now?" Bonnie asked. "Do we try to get her out of here?"

Fargo looked at the beaten, scarred, seared body. "No way. She can't be moved. Christ, she's hardly alive. Moving her could finish her." Bonnie's question hung in her eyes. "We wait," he said. "Wait, watch. It's not over. Move in when the moment's right."

"What if they start on her again? I couldn't stand by," Bonnie said.

He nodded with his mouth a thin line. "They start on her again and we move on them. There are three dead men who don't know they're dead yet." He paused at Nellie, tried to get through to the battered figure again, gave up and stalked from the house. He returned to where they had left the horses.

"Why this far back?" Bonnie asked.

"Till it gets dark," he said, settled down. She frowned at him, plainly not satisfied with his answer but aware that she'd get no other one. She leaned against him and he felt the shudder go through her.

"Why? What would they want so bad they'd do that? What kind of animals are they?"

"Humans, not animals Animals don't do things like that," Fargo said.

"Then they're monsters," Bonnie said fiercely. "Monsters or madmen."

"Or both."

"They still had some reason, twisted, mad reason."

"I'd guess money. Greed. It can turn people into monsters. I've seen it do it before, too damn often."

"It still makes no sense."

"There are a lot of holes yet but I can put some of it together," Fargo said. "Judge Counsil had to be part of it, a key part."

"With the sheriff, Smith and Evans?"

"With all of them. Something happened. Trouble, disagreements, or maybe the others thought he was pulling out on them. Whatever, they killed the judge and pinned it on Nellie Noonan. They gave out the story about the affair to give her a motive."

"Only they didn't hang her," Bonnie said. "They hung Carrie in her place. Why?"

"They needed Nellie. They thought she knew something they had to know, something the judge took with him when they killed him. That's why they've been torturing her."

"But what?"

He shrugged. "That's one of the holes."

"Where did Joe Holder fit in? How does an undertaker figure into it?"

"That's one of the holes too."

"He had to be part of their switching Carrie for Nellie. Maybe they killed him to stop him from telling you that," Bonnie offered.

"Maybe, and maybe there was more to his part."

"What'd the sheriff send them all out looking for?" Bonnie frowned.

"I told you there were a lot of holes," Fargo said. She started to answer when he put a finger to her lips and she froze into silence. The two figures appeared in moments, moving through the trees toward the house, the sheriff and Smith. The others came into sight soon after as dusk began to turn the woods dark gray.

"We move closer now?" Bonnie asked.

"We stay here and be quiet," Fargo said. She frowned and sat back against a tree. Night settled in quickly, the woods turning black until the moon came up enough to allow its pale light to filter in. The light from the house glowed through the trees and muffled voices echoed in the stillness.

"I keep waiting for a scream." Bonnie shuddered.

"I don't think she can scream much anymore," Fargo said.

"Don't you think we ought to move in closer again?"

"No." His voice shut off further questions. He heard her impatience as she moved, shifted position.

The moon rose higher, sent in a little more light and Fargo's eyes were half closed, his head back against a hemlock. He guessed another half hour had gone by when his eyes snapped fully open and the sound of the horse, moving slowly, came through the trees from the pathway a few feet away. He felt Bonnie's hand dig into his arm. He squeezed her hand reassuringly as he rose to his feet, the Colt in his hand and the rider appeared, a dark shadow moving toward him along the path. He waited till the rider drew closer, began to take definite shape. He stepped into the path and the horse halted.

"Come on forward, Mariel," Fargo said, and heard Bonnie's gasp of surprise, saw her pull herself to her feet out of the corner of his eye. The horse moved and came into plain view, Mariel Counsil in the saddle, a cape around her shoulders. "Been waiting for you, Mariel," Fargo said softly.

The woman stared at him and a tiny smile played

around the corners of her lips. "You didn't know all along. Don't tell me that," she said.

"No, you took me in—hook, line and sinker. You were good, set it up better than I've ever seen done, being so honest, agreeing with what I suspected, proving yourself by springing me out of jail. It was good, real good. One reason it worked was that half of it was true."

Mariel Counsil's smile grew wider, took on a wry candor. "What do you mean half of it was true?" he heard Bonnie ask.

Fargo's eyes stayed on Mariel Counsil as he answered. "The judge hadn't given it to her in five years. That's why she knew there was no affair between him and Nellie. She proved that to me," Fargo said. "Beyond a doubt. Some lips can lie. Some can't."

"Bastard," he heard Bonnie breathe.

Mariel's smile stayed and her pale tan eyes seemed quietly amused as she kept them on the big man in front of her. "What made you decide about me?" she asked.

"Two things. They nagged at me and all I knew was that something didn't fit. I wasn't sure until I went to the cemetery and then they stopped nagging and took shape. The grave had been dug up. They saw the box opened, and knew I knew the truth about that much. I kept wondering what made them decide to dig it open and then I realized they'd dug because you told them to look, to make sure."

"But you didn't actually tell me you'd seen Carrie Akins there," Mariel said in mock protest.

"I told you enough to make you nervous," Fargo said. "And there was one more thing. You sent Treeman with that note about Evans coming to see you. But I forgot to tell you I was staying at Bonnie's place. The only way you could've known that was because Coleman told you and that meant you were really working together." Mariel Counsil shrugged. Fargo's voice grew harsh. "I saw Nellie. You're a part of it. You'll pay with the others."

"They went too far. I never told them to do that much to her," Mariel Counsil protested.

"I don't believe you, honey," Fargo said. "But first I want you to fill in the rest."

Her smile stayed. "Go to hell, big man," she said.

"Talk or you'll be the first to pay for Nellie," Fargo warned. "You made a mistake by not bringing that goddamn giant along."

"But I did." The woman smiled. "He's right behind you, with a rifle at your back."

Fargo turned slowly and saw the treelike figure just behind him, saw Bonnie's wide-eyed glance back also.

"Drop your gun, Fargo," Mariel Counsil said. "Treeman will blast you if I lift my finger, though he'd much prefer killing you with his bare hands. He always follows a dozen yards behind me. He saw you stop me, circled around and came up behind you. For all his size, he's silent as a ghost."

"Seems so," Fargo said as he let the Colt fall from his fingers.

"You move now," a deep, guttural voice boomed and the giant figure came forward. Fargo stepped aside and the man picked up the Colt, pushed it into his belt.

"Let's go, to the house," Mariel said. Fargo turned, felt Bonnie against his side as she started for the house with him. Mariel rode ahead as they neared the house, swung from the horse and Fargo saw the sheriff and Evans step outside, their eyes growing wide.

"Jesus, where'd they come from?" Coleman frowned.

"Outside. You stupid bastards never do anything right," Mariel Counsil hissed. "Bring them inside." She strode into the house and Fargo followed with Bonnie, the sheriff eyeing Fargo with malevolent triumph.

"Last stop for you, Fargo," he said. "This time it's all over for you. Her too," he added, nodding at Bonnie. He barked orders at one of the hired hands. "Get their horses and hitch them outside." The hired hand hurried from the house. The giant figure moved to one side of the room, his head almost touching the ceiling, his gaunt face expressionless. Only the coal-black eyes glittered as he looked at Bonnie.

"He work on Nellie?" Fargo asked, his eyes blue steel.

"Some," Mariel said. "I'm still amazed she didn't talk."

"She didn't talk because she doesn't know anything, you stinkin' bitch," Fargo exploded. "You said yourself she wasn't having an affair with him. He didn't tell her whatever the hell you want to find out."

"What we want to find out is where he's been burying the money," the woman flung back, sudden anger flaring in her. "I told you he didn't have an affair but he did see himself as a father to her. He told her everything, fawned on her, considered her his damn daughter."

"Not everything. She couldn't have held out. She doesn't have that kind of strength," Fargo said.

"We knew he was getting ready to take off with her

and the money," the woman said. "I still think she knows where it is."

"What money?" Fargo pressed.

"The money he's been taking on the side for twenty years, bribe money, payoffs not to hang somebody, money given him to go light or go heavy. He was circuit judge. He controlled everything. In Brushville, Tim, Charley and the sheriff worked with him. He had others in other towns, other places. He told them he'd split with them when the time came."

Sheriff Coleman cut in. "We figure he's buried some twenty thousand dollars over the years."

"He means *buried*," the woman said. "When he got enough together, he'd have Joe Holder meet him with one of his pine boxes and he'd go off to see over a funeral someplace. Only the box would be filled with money. He was smart. He made sure nobody followed him and saw where he went. He didn't bury the boxes in the Brushville cemetery. He couldn't have kept that quiet. It had to be some little, out-of-the-way cemetery someplace."

"And you think he told Nellie," Fargo said. "You bitch, you stupid, stinkin' bitch."

Mariel Counsil stepped forward, smashed her hand across his face. "Bastard," she hissed.

"I hope you never find it," Fargo said.

"You won't live to know," the woman snarled. "Tie him; the girl too."

Two of the hired hands quickly obeyed with a length of lariat. Fargo tightened his powerful arm and wrist muscles as he felt the ropes put around him, binding him to a straight-backed chair. He let his forearm bulge out as the man hurriedly wrapped the rope around his arms, kept his muscles tight until the man finished and stepped back. He relaxed his body then, felt the slight give in the ropes. Not much, but enough, he hoped. If there was time left. His eyes found Bonnie, saw her frowning at him, thoughts racing through her mind. She frowned at him but she seemed preoccupied, lost in her own thoughts as the other man finished tying her to the chair.

"Revive the Noonan bitch," Mariel Counsil ordered. "Try her again."

"I don't believe she can take any more," the mayor said and looked uncomfortable.

"Try, dammit. This is no time to get squeamish," the woman barked. "Douse her with water and get her awake. Treeman will do the rest."

Fargo's eyes went to the giant, saw the man's long face seem to take on a flicker of anticipation. One of the hands brought in a bucket of water and the sheriff and Evans went down the hall with it. Fargo's eyes burned into Mariel Counsil. He felt the rage inside him, the worst kind, helpless, gut-tearing rage. He tore his eyes from the woman, knew the muscles in his neck were straining, bulging as the frustrated fury consumed him. He drew a deep breath. He was helpless and he had to stay in control. He couldn't try to get free now, not with all the others watching. He looked at Bonnie. She was staring at the floor, the little frown still on her forehead, still immersed in her own racing thoughts.

Fargo heard the tiny, whimpered sound come from the other end of the hall. Mariel nodded at the giant. "Go on," she ordered. "Maybe she's had enough to talk finally."

Fargo put his head down, pressed his eyes shut

and wished he could do the same with his ears as the tiny, whimpered sound came again. She'd never live through more, he thought helplessly, never.

"Leave her alone." The words cut through the air, Bonnie's voice, almost a scream and he lifted his head, saw her staring at Mariel Counsil.

"Shut up," the woman snapped disdainfully.

"Leave her alone," Bonnie repeated. "I think I know the cemetery."

6

Fargo stared at Bonnie with a combination of disbelief and despair. The room fell silent and Fargo saw Mariel Counsil's eyes fastened on Bonnie as a cat fastens on a mouse. Sheriff Coleman thrust his face forward at Bonnie's bound, helpless form in the chair. "You're a goddamn lying little bitch," he snarled.

Mariel stepped closer, brushed the sheriff aside, her eyes still pinned on the girl in the chair. "Do you mean that or are you just trying to buy time?"

"I mean it," Bonnie said. "I think I know the cemetery you want."

"She's lying. How could she," Coleman barked.

Fargo watched as Mariel Counsil speared him with a gaze of pure contempt. "Close your stupid mouth," she hissed. "You haven't done one thing right so far. Don't you dare to give me orders." The sheriff's face reddened and Fargo saw the man's lips twitch but he backed away. Smith and Evans looked on unhappily but they were plainly not about to take issue with the woman.

A sharp, brief cry of anguish came from the end room, Nellie's pitiful gasp of renewed pain. "Stop him. Stop him," Bonnie screamed. "Stop him or I don't tell you anything."

Mariel Counsil flicked a finger at Evans and the banker down the hall to the room. The woman's eyes stayed on Bonnie. "Talk," she said.

"No, oh, no, not just like that. We agree, first. I'll tell you what I know if you let us go, Nellie Noonan too," Bonnie said, and Fargo felt the amazement circling inside him. Fools rushing in where angels fear to tread, he thought to himself.

"We don't have to make any deal with you," the woman said. "You know something? We'll let Treeman get it out of you."

"He won't," Bonnie snapped back, and Fargo stared at her, hardly able to believe his ears. "I can't stand pain. I hurt bad and I faint. It's always been that way, something that just happens. All he'll get out of me is fainting." Fargo saw Mariel Counsil's eyes bore into Bonnie. "But I think I know your cemetery," Bonnie said.

The woman flicked a glance at the three men. "Let's talk," she said, and the three followed her into the adjoining room.

Fargo leaned as close to Bonnie as his bonds would allow. "You crazy?" he hissed.

"About the fainting? It's true," she said. "Since I was a little girl. I pass out and stay out."

"About everything, dammit. You can't get away with some crazy story," Fargo hissed at her.

"I'm not trying to. I'm pretty sure I know," she said. He wanted to say more but the figures emerged from the other room, Mariel Counsil first, and he leaned back, pulled at the ropes binding him. Because he had bulged out his muscles when he was bound, the ropes weren't absolutely tight and now he flexed his muscles, tried to loosen them further. Mariel faced Bonnie, the three men looking on.

"We've agreed. You give us something real and you live," the woman said.

Fargo groaned inwardly as Bonnie nodded agreement. "You'll stick to it," she said.

"Of course," the woman said, and Fargo groaned silently again. "Talk," Mariel Counsil snapped out sharply.

Bonnie drew a deep breath. "Near where I used to live, in Owlseville, there's a place called Elder Mountain," she began.

"I know where it is," the sheriff interjected. "Been past it."

"Halfway around the foot of Elder Mountain there's a small cemetery. Only the folks that live around the mountain know about it and use it, the Hollymans, the Kecklers, the Rudolphs and a few more more big families. It's not their cemetery but they're the only ones who use it, except for the judge."

"The judge?" Evans echoed.

"I used to see him coming back from there in the early mornings, always alone, always driving a spring wagon with cut-under wheels," Bonnie said.

Fargo watched the sheriff's jaw drop. "That's what he drove, a spring wagon with cut-under wheels," the man exclaimed. "By Christ maybe she does know."

"Goddamn, it fits," the mayor said excitedly.

"Go on, dearie," Mariel Counsil said to Bonnie.

"Once, I saw him in the evening, carrying something long and covered in the wagon," Bonnie said. "It never meant anything to me till now, when you started talking about his burying money in pine caskets. But I used to see him often enough."

"How often?" the sheriff asked.

"Every few months, I'd guess."

"That's it. Everything fits. Goddamn, we've got it," the mayor shouted, and Fargo watched the exchange of glee among the trio. Mariel's lips pursed and in her face there was only cold triumph.

"Get the horses. Take something to eat on the way. We want to make time," the woman ordered. "It'll be dawn in a few hours and we'll be on the way."

The others hurried off to do as they were told and Mariel gathered the cape around her shoulders. "What about us?" Fargo heard Bonnie ask.

Mariel Counsil's slow smile was made of icy malevolence. She turned to the towering, gaunt figure standing by the wall. "They're yours, Treeman. Kill them when you're finished."

Fargo watched as Bonnie's eyes grew wide, her lips dropping open and then the frown digging into her brow. "Bitch. Lying, rotten bitch," Bonnie shouted at the woman.

"Fool. Stupid little fool," Mariel Counsil flung back with disdain, swung the cape around as she strode out of the house with the towering figure following her. Bonnie's gaze went to Fargo, hurt and anger in it.

"I'd say you were both right," he commented grimly.

"Thanks," Bonnie threw back bitterly, fell silent for a minute, then flared again. "I thought they'd keep their bargain. Maybe I was a fool but I tried to get us out."

"You did. You didn't hurt us any. They figured to kill us anyway. Nothing's changed." Fargo's eyes went to the door as the figure entered, filled the doorway and had to duck its head to step through. Treeman's coal-black eyes glittered as they focused on Bonnie

140

and Fargo strained arm muscles as he tried to make the bonds give further. But they held his arms stretched firmly around the back of the straight-backed chair. He saw Treeman step toward Bonnie and his eyes swept the room. He'd have little time, he realized, very little time. But the almost bare room offered nothing, not a nail, not even a sharp stone corner on which he could rub the ropes. Treeman had reached Bonnie and once again Fargo knew the terrible rage of helplessness. Bonnie's eyes had turned to fear as the towering figure leered down at her. Fargo's eyes swept the room again and he halted as he saw, at the edge of the fireplace, a big iron hook on which to hang kettles. His eyes went back to Bonnie as the huge figure stood in front of her.

"You and Treeman have good time first," the figure rumbled. Fargo watched Treeman reach one long arm out, pull Bonnie and the chair forward, reach behind it and untie the ropes binding the girl. Bonnie dived forward instantly, fell on her knees, tried to get up and run but Treeman spun, seized her with one huge hand, picked her up and held her under one arm as though she were a child. A harsh, guttural sound came from him that somehow managed to convey glee as he started down the hallway with Bonnie. Fargo saw the man disappear into the room nearest the last one that held Nellie. He rose, bent over with the chair strapped to him, hobbled to the edge of the fireplace, backed up against the big hook. He maneuvered, missed, finally got the hook into the space between his wrists and the rope where the point dug into the rope.

He heard a heavy crash as Treeman threw Bonnie onto a bed. "No . . . no!" he heard Bonnie scream.

The rumbling roar of Treeman's voice drowned out her second scream and he heard sounds of scuffling, footsteps slipping. He glimpsed Bonnie dart out the door, her blouse torn from her, only to be pulled back into the room. Fargo swore as he pushed his wrists against the hook, ignored the pain as he rubbed the ropes back and forth over the hook that also tore into his skin. He could hear Bonnie was still fighting and Treeman's roars growing louder and angrier. Suddenly one wrist came loose and he felt the rope tearing, giving way. He yanked hard and the other wrist came free. He pulled both arms out from behind the chair, kicked the chair back into the empty fireplace and raced down the hallway, rubbing circulation back into his arms as he ran.

He skidded around the doorway into the room, saw Bonnie naked, on a double-sized mattress on the floor. Treeman lay atop her, holding her by the throat with one hand, but she twisted and turned her legs and torso and he roared in anger and lust as his thrusts kept missing their mark. He halted, turned around as Fargo raced into the room. Treeman's trousers were still hanging open, and Fargo stared for a moment at an organ that belonged on a horse. Treeman pushed himself up, his mouth opening in a guttural roar of fury and Fargo saw Bonnie roll from the mattress. The man started toward him, his tremendous, bestial organ hanging, then disappearing inside his open trousers. Fargo crouched, let the towering figure charge, stepped to one side as Treeman hurtled at him. He threw a tremendous right into the side of the man's ribs, a blow that would have felled most opponents with smashed ribs. Treeman stumbled, grunted, whirled to face his attacker and Fargo stepped in with two hard blows to the midsection. Treeman took a step back and Fargo stepped in to smash another blow into the man's middle when a treelike arm came up, blocked the blow and the towering figure leaped forward. Fargo tried to duck to the side but the huge form smashed into him and he felt himself go down. Tremendous hands closed around him and he felt himself being lifted off the ground, whirled and flung into the air. He smashed against the wall, felt his body shudder in a spasm of overwhelming pain.

He shook his head as purple-and-yellow dots flashed before his eyes, felt himself sliding to the floor against the wall. He just managed to see the huge foot hurtling at him, flung himself sideways and took only half the force of the kick. Yet it sent him rolling across the floor to smash into the opposite wall. He saw Treeman charging across the room at him, shook away pain and sprang to his feet, stepped to the right and avoided the man's arcing blow. He stepped under the huge arm, brought up a tremendous uppercut that landed flush on the point of the long, hanging jaw. Treeman grunted, blinked, rocked a half step backward and Fargo crossed a left to his jaw. The towering figure took another step backward, let out an earth-shattering roar and brought both huge arms up at once, striking out with both.

Fargo avoided the one, took the other on his shoulder and rocked backward. Treeman leaped at him again, arms outstretched and Fargo ducked down, tried to smash in another blow but it only scraped along the side of the gaunt face. Treeman hurled his towering form sideways, the move quick and unexpected and Fargo felt himself flung against the wall. The long arms came up to catch him around the waist and again he felt himself lifted clear off the ground. He wrapped his arms around the man's head, squeezed and heard Treeman grunt, pain in the sound. But the man slammed him against the wall with bone-shattering force and Fargo felt the wave of pain shoot through his body. Treeman dropped him, stepped back and Fargo again slid to the floor. But this time, the huge figure's kick landed and Fargo gasped in pain as the blow caught him in the small of the back. He felt a gray curtain come over his eyes, shook his head and the curtain lifted. But he was being pulled halfway, lifted again and he felt himself flung through the air. Treeman's toss went bad and Fargo hit the mattress, bounced, came onto his feet. He saw Bonnie, her skirt on, holding one of the straight-backed chairs. She charged at Treeman from behind as the huge figure rushed toward the mattress and Fargo stepped to the firm footing of the floor, saw her smash the chair into Treeman. She reached up, tried to bring the chair down onto the back of the man's head but succeeded only in smashing it against his shoulder blades. Treeman let out a roar of more fury than pain, whirled as the chair broke into pieces. His back-handed blow caught Bonnie alongside the shoulder and sent her flying across the room to land in a heap against the wall.

Fargo charged and Treeman spun, lashed out with another backhanded blow. The Trailsman ducked under it, used every ounce of power in his shoulders to drive a straight right into the man's jaw. Treeman staggered back a pace and Fargo followed with a tremendous left hook to the long jaw. The huge figure staggered back again, dropped its arms and Fargo stepped in to bring up another blow. But Treeman lunged forward, the blow landing harm-

144

lessly against his chest. Fargo tried to twist away from the long arms that came up but his foot slipped and he stumbled, felt the blow that smashed into the side of his head. No numbing sharpness to it but a pile-driver power that sent him to the floor. He glimpsed the man's knee came up, tried to twist aside but the blow caught him in the side and he groaned in pain as his breath seemed to fly from him. He doubled over, felt the huge hands around his neck, the pressure instant. He got his own hands around one of the man's wrists, pulled and gave up, felt breath and strength giving out on him.

He reached down, groped with his hand as Tree-man's black coal eyes glittered over him and the huge hands squeezed his throat. Only a tiny trickle of air escaped him now, and Fargo felt the dizziness take hold, then the sudden pounding in his temples. His hand felt the calf holster finally and he drew the thin, double-edged blade. He could feel the strength draining from him as his last few breaths rasped through his throat. His arm came up as though it were underwater, a maddening slowness to it. He plunged the knife into the man's side and heard Treeman's surprised half grunt, half gasp. The hands left his throat and Treeman pulled back, got to his feet. Fargo rolled away, gulped in great drafts of air as he lay on his stomach. He looked up to see the towering figure yank the knife from his side, stare at it for an instant and fling it away. Fargo's curses echoed inside him. The blade hadn't gone in far, had hit nothing vital. He saw Treeman start for him again, the gaunt face now a twisted, hollow-cheeked mask of hate. Bonnie, in one corner, was slowly pulling herself to her feet, Fargo noticed as he rose, prepared to meet the man's charge.

His body burned, pain coursing through every part of it, sapping his remaining strength. He measured the onrushing figure, ducked a wild swing from one polelike arm, brought up another smashing uppercut to the long jaw. They'd all been blows that would have taken out most men and Treeman staggered back, swayed, rushed forward again. Fargo felt the pain in his wrist and arm from the crashing blows he'd delivered, stepped away from another wild swing of the long arms, threw a sharp left hook to the jaw. Again the man halted, shook away the blow and came on. Fargo ducked under Treeman's swinging arms but held back a blow, raced for the door instead. He needed a weapon, a club, something to do what his depleted strength couldn't do. Hitting the giant was like hitting a tree with one's bare fist. He reached the front door, raced outside as he heard the thudding footsteps close behind him.

He plunged across the few yards of clear space and into the trees, bulled through the brush, hands and eyes seeking, groping. He saw the figure come after him, looking as though a tree had sprouted feet and given chase. Fargo cursed in desperation. He had seen the piece of fallen tree as he'd lain in wait earlier, broken branches alongside it. He whirled, changed directions and knew the pursuing figure was closing in on him, each long-legged stride equaling three of his own. He scanned the forest floor as he ran, eyes leaping over shadowed shapes barely touched by moonlight and then he glimpsed it, a dozen yards away, the dark length of fallen tree. He felt the figure coming up at his heels, spun, started to streak for the log when a sledgehammer blow caught him in the small of his back and he went down with a gasp of pain that seared, drove the breath from his body. He tried to roll but Treeman was upon him, brought down another hammerlike blow. It hit Fargo alongside the temple, drove his face into the ground.

Fargo felt himself being turned onto his back, his body consumed with pain and he saw the huge arm drawn back to bring down another bone-crushing blow. He managed to get both arms up and block the blow but the force of it drove his right forearm to his face. He lay there, felt his own powerful muscles grown weak with pain and exhaustion, hardly able to respond. He kept his arms up to protect his face and felt the man's huge hands pulling them aside. The long-jawed, brutal face hung over him. The man was a monster, a monster of insensate strength and insensate cruelty and Nellie Noonan's tortured, burned, whipped body swam into his mind. Fargo felt the surge of rage spiral, summoning up a last gasp of strength out of his own hate. He brought his fist around in a looping blow, kept his thumb extended as he drove the blow into one glittering eye.

"Aaaaaagh . . ." the man bellowed, reared back, clapped one hand to his eye and Fargo dove forward, kicked out, landed a foot in the man's belly and rolled. He reached the log, closed his hands around a clublike length of branch. Treeman was charging again. "Kill you. Kill you," the towering figure screamed as he rushed forward. Fargo set himself, crouched, the heavy length of branch in his hands. Treeman saw the weapon, brought both polelike arms up to form an effective shield and came on, increased his headlong charge. Fargo dropped low, swung the piece of wood with all his remaining strength and smashed it across the man's knees. He heard the kneebones shatter and Treeman toppled forward with a roar of pain. He rolled on his side, long arms reaching down to clasp his knees.

Fargo stepped in with the branch held upraised with both hands, brought it down with all his strength. It smashed into the man's skull and broke in half. But Fargo saw the man fall backward, his jaw hanging open. Using half of the branch, Fargo brought the jagged end down into the man's throat, pulled it free and a half-dozen red spouts erupted. Treeman made gargled noises, clutched at his throat, rolled, started to get to his feet and collapsed as his broken kneecaps gave way. Fargo smashed the branch across his face, heard his nose snap. He smashed it down again and again until there was no face, only a smear of red. "For Nellie, you stinkin' monster," Fargo heard himself gasp out. "For Nellie."

He brought the piece of branch down in a final smashing blow, stepped back, saw Treeman a still figure, looking not unlike a bloodied log. Fargo staggered back and the piece of branch slipped out of his fingers as his arm dropped to his side. He felt the last ounce of strength drain from his battered, aching body. The dizziness returned, swept over him and he sank down on his knees, then onto the ground. The grayness descended and he closed his eyes. The still, night forest vanished away.

He woke to coolness on his forehead and felt smooth skin on his face. He pulled his eyelids open. He was still in the woods, he noted almost abstractly, the dark, wavy shapes of tree branches over his head. A face came into view, bending low over him, plump cheeks, brown eyes darkened with concern. "Thank God," Bonnie said as she looked into his opened eyes.

"I wondered if you'd ever wake up. I thought maybe you had a concussion."

"No concussion but damn near dead," he muttered, felt his forehead with one hand and found the cold, wet cloth there.

"I waited inside until it grew still, then I came out looking. God, I was so afraid of what I found. When I couldn't wake you I went in and soaked the cloth in water."

Fargo struggled up on his elbows and his body cried out, every part of it sore and bruised, it seemed. He looked over at the inert, prone form on the ground.

"He's done," Bonnie said, and Fargo started to push himself to his feet and welcomed Bonnie's helping hand. He straightened, drew a deep breath and thought his ribs were going to fall off. "Can you ride?"

"Slowly," he said.

"What now?"

"We find a doc for Nellie, see that she's in his hands and then go after them." Fargo saw Bonnie's face grow still; his eyes narrowed.

"Nellie won't be needing a doc, Fargo," she said softly. "When I went back to get the cold cloth for you, I looked in on her. The last try they made was too much for her."

Fargo strode from her, ignored the pain in his body as he hurried into the house. He halted at the doorway of the room, his eyes staring at the bed. Bonnie had drawn a sheet over most of the still, small form and Fargo's jaw grew hard, his eyes blue stone. "We'll take her with us, find a nice place somewhere," he said, and Bonnie nodded.

"I'll get the horses," she said, and as she did, he

retrieved the knife where Treeman had flung it and found his Colt. He saw Bonnie come to the outside door with the horses, turned and went back into the last room. When he emerged, he carried the small figure carefully shrouded in two sheets. He laid Nellie Noonan over his saddle, swung onto the Ovaro beside her. Bonnie rode a few paces behind as dawn sent pink streaks across the sky. Fargo rode in silence as the new day came and it was late morning when he halted at the side of a hill that looked down on a lush, green valley.

"Here," he said as he gently took Nellie from across the saddle. Bonnie helped him scoop out a shallow place, put her in it and form a sturdy cover of rocks. He erected a small cross out of tree branches, stood in silence before the simple grave when they finished. "They'll pay, every last one of them," he murmured. "I promise you. And Carrie." He turned, swung into the saddle and his silence now was made of vengeance as much as grief. They'd ridden into the afternoon when Bonnie called to him as she reined up.

"I know a short cut," she said, and his eyes questioned. She pointed up across a small mountain to their right.

"Over there?" He frowned.

"There's a path. I'd an uncle who used to go that way. They've a good start on us. They could get there, dig up their damned money and clear out. I don't want that."

He thought for a moment. Her fears weren't realistic. The others wouldn't make that much time on them. Yet it was just possible. "All right, let's go," he said crisply. It was nearing dark when they reached the small mountain and the trail up and he made

150

camp beneath a stand of junipers. He undressed to underpants and slid into his bedroll. His brows lifted as he saw Bonnie preparing her own bedroll. "Not coming over?" he asked.

"Doesn't look like it, does it?"

"I see. Thought I could get a back rub. I could sure use one." She made no reply. He rose onto one elbow. "Mind telling me why you're staying over there?"

"I don't have to prove anything," she said tartly.

"So that's it," Fargo said.

"That's it," Bonnie returned. "You didn't have to sleep with her just because she wanted to prove herself to you. How does it feel knowing you made love to someone like that?"

"I had some chili one night that made me real sick later. I hated it then but I sure enjoyed it while I was eating it," he said and lay back. "Sleep tight."

"Animal," she hissed.

Fargo turned on his side, winced with the pain of his still-sore back where the sledgehammer blow had all but cracked him in two. He closed his eyes, had drawn but a few deep and painful breaths when he heard the soft sound of her footsteps, felt her slide into the bedroll, her nakedness warm against his flesh. "You change your mind fast," he said.

"I didn't change my mind. I brought some of your salve to rub in," she said. "Strictly a good deed. Turn over."

He turned onto his stomach and enjoyed the soft touch of her hands as she rubbed the salve into his sore muscles. "Turn over," she said again when she finished, and he turned onto his back. The salve was working already, his muscles relaxing. He felt Bonnie's hands moving over his chest, no salve now, move

151

down his rib cage, over his abdomen, push his shorts away and curl around his organ. He had often marveled how the body can operate in sections as part of him still ached but now another part sprang into eager life. Bonnie's hands stroked, caressed and he heard her tiny cries of delight as he thickened, grew, began to throb in her hand. He started to move, bring her down to him but she pushed him back. "No, let me," she said, stretched herself over his legs, moved down, rubbed her breasts with his throbbing eagerness and cried out as she pressed each nipple onto its pulsating warmth. She drew her legs up, slid onto him and uttered a groan of pleasure. Mindful of his aching body, she made love to him with a gentleness that was both soothing and exciting, finally pressing herself down onto him until he could go no further inside her and her climax brought a breathy scream as she lay atop him with knees drawn up, rocked back and forth and whimpered little sounds of ecstasy. She stayed holding him in her long after the sweet moment had come and gone, finally drawing her legs down and sliding from him to lie across his chest.

"Strictly good deed?" he remarked.

"I didn't say for whom," she answered, her voice already thick with sleep, and he held her, let the night envelop their sleeping forms.

When morning came she rode beside him up the pathway that led high into the small mountain. The land grew higher, more wild and he frowned as the path continued to stay flattened down. "This is a damn well-worn trail for a place this wild and this high up," he muttered. "Must be used by mountain men and trappers." He looked at Bonnie and she made no comment. He rode on, scanned the sides of the trail but saw no discarded traps, no sign of trap lines anywhere. His frown stayed as he noted a lot of unshod Indian pony tracks, most dried out, moving along the trail and crisscrossing it from both sides of the timbered mountain land. His frown deepened as he reined up, bent low in the saddle and picked up a broken arrow. "Northern Shoshones," he said, studying the marks at the base of the shaft. He let the broken arrow drop to the ground and rode on.

He reined up again a half mile higher along the trail, dismounted this time to pick up a piece of a parfleche lying along one edge of the trail. He studied the triangle pattern of colors that had been dyed into it. "Kiowa," he muttered, cast a glance at Bonnie. She stayed silent, seemed to wait with thinly veiled impatience. He remounted and rode on and Bonnie stayed silent as she rode alongside him. The trail continued to climb into the wild mountain land and continued to stay well worn. Fargo suddenly reined the Ovaro to another halt as he swung from the horses beside a small area of flattened brush beside the trail. The remains of two horned owls lay on the ground and he knelt down, examined both. The tail feathers and the talons had been plucked from each.

He rose, fastened Bonnie with a hard eye. "This is a goddamn Indian hunting trail, isn't it?" he said. She said nothing. "They all use it and you knew it," he barked. She continued to stay silent. "You practice doing damn fool things?"

Her face was set as she turned her eyes on him. "I told you, I want to get there before they have a chance to clear out."

"You stick your hand in a hornet's nest to get honey?" Fargo snapped. She tossed a glare back. "Indians don't like anyone on their lands. They especially don't like anyone on their private hunting grounds. Even the mountain men stay clear of some places."

"My uncle used to come this way. We'll make it."

"Used to?" Fargo asked, picking up on her phrase. "What happened to him?"

"He set out and never came back one time." She met Fargo's angry exasperation with a glower. "All right, then let's not waste time talking about it. Let's get on."

Fargo's eyes moved past her and he felt the muscle in his jaw throb. "You may not be getting on anywhere," he murmured. Bonnie spun in the saddle to follow his gaze and saw the line of near-naked, bronze-skinned figures moving on their ponies across the trail, not more than a few hundred yards away. Fargo backed the Ovaro under a tree and pulled Bonnie's horse in by the checkstrap. "Kiowa," he whispered. "They didn't see us."

Bonnie watched through the trees with him as the Indians halted. One at the end carried a half-dozen marten and beaver skins. "A hunting party," Bonnie said.

"They'll be happy to add us," Fargo answered. The leader, wearing a beaded headband, slowly turned his horse in a complete circle. He turned again, halted as he faced down the trail. With a sudden shout to the others, he led the charge down the trail.

"I thought you said they didn't see us," Bonnie said.

"They didn't. They smell us. Leather and saddle soap, white-man smell," Fargo said. He reached out, drew the big Spencer out of Bonnie's saddle case. "Run for it, down the trail."

Her eyes stared at him. "They'll catch me in minutes," she protested.

"Both of us if I go with you," he said. "You're decoy. Move out." Her eyes said she understood and that didn't make it any better. Fargo backed the Ovaro deeper into the trees as Bonnie bolted down the trail. He saw the Kiowa gallop past seconds later, heard Bonnie's scream a moment after and then the excited shouts of the young bucks. He stayed back, letting his ears tell him what took place. After more excited shouts, a roar of harsh laughter, the bucks settled down and Fargo heard them moving back up the trail. They passed where he hid in the trees and he saw they had hold of Bonnie's horse, one brave leading it, another behind. No thongs binding Bonnie's wrists, he noted. They were a confident lot.

He let them go far enough up the trail before he edged from the trees. He followed at a safe distance, stayed in the trees and kept downwind of the hunting party. He counted on their bringing their captive back to their man camp untouched, to show her off before enjoying her. The camp could be days away and he hadn't days to wait. He continued to follow, staying to one side as the Indians moved along the trail. They were talkative as well as confident, kept up a chatter unlike most Indians. But then the Kiowa were known to be talkative. He wished he understood their tongue, knowing only a few phrases.

Many of the plains tribes spoke a version of common language. The Crow, Dakota, Assiniboin, Osage and a dozen others all spoke the Siouan tongue. The Cheyenne, Arapaho and Blackfoot were among those who spoke Algonquian. The Ute, northern Shoshones, Bannock and some Comanche spoke dialects of the

Shoshonean tongue and he had learned enough of each of those. But the Kiowa had their own language and he listened, tried to pick up a word and understood nothing. They continued to ride the trail and he took a grim satisfaction from that. The sun had moved into the afternoon sky when they veered from the trail and the heat to ride into the cool of the timberland. Fargo halted, watched, saw the six braves halt, slide down from their ponies. The leader with the headband pulled Bonnie from her horse, yanked her around and tied her wrists behind her with a length of rawhide. He pulled her to the trunk of a young, thin fir and tied her to it with a length of rope. Probably some poor cowhand's last lariat, Fargo thought. He saw the brave find a comfortable spot on the ground and lie down. The others did the same and Fargo swore under his breath.

He had counted on night and darkness to go in after Bonnie but they had crossed him up. They were taking their sleep in the heat of the late afternoon. They plainly figured to ride during the night. "Damn," he swore, settled himself on the ground and waited as he tried to find a way to save Bonnie. Sneaking in as he'd planned to do was almost suicide now. They'd wake, he expected that even at night, but then he'd have had the cover of darkness as an ally. In the daylight he'd be an easy target when they woke. There'd be no chance to cut Bonnie loose and lose themselves in the night timberland. He swore again. He was left with no options but to go in and get her.

He rose, took his big Sharps from its saddle holster, Bonnie's old Spencer in the other hand and started toward the sleeping Kiowa on noiseless steps. There'd be no sneaking in. He couldn't risk getting caught trying to cut Bonnie free. He had to strike hard, fast and effectively, cut down the odds in one instant move. He'd have no time for more than that first, surprise strike. He moved closer, heard the sounds of snoring. Bonnie stood against the tree, her head hanging down. Fargo dropped to the ground, began to crawl forward, a rifle in each hand, inching his way noiselessly. He halted when he was as close as he dared come to the sleeping bucks and swept the figures with a narrowed glance. Two lay near each other at the left, one not too far from them. Two more slept on the other side of the small area and the leader lay not far from Bonnie.

Fargo took the Sharps first, resting it on the ground and sighted along the long barrel, drew a bead on one of the nearest two sleeping figures. He steadied the rifle in place with two rocks, sighted along it again, made sure it was on target. He took the old Spencer, next, did the same, this time on the second sleeping form. He raised the barrel a fraction to allow for the Indian sitting up instantly. A piece of rotted branch and a rock served to steady the Spencer in position and once again he sighted along the rifle to be certain it stayed on target after he steadied it with the rock. He lay prone, took the Colt out and placed it on the ground at his fingertips. He stretched both arms out, curled his left forefinger around the trigger of the Spencer, his right around the trigger of his big Sharps.

He took a final sighting along each rifle. There'd be no chance for a second try. It had to go off like clockwork the first time. He cast a quick glance at the Colt on the ground, moved it up six inches closer to the Sharps. He was returning his hand to the trigger of the rifle when the Indian sat bolt upright

157

and Fargo swore. The Kiowa hadn't heard anything. Intuition had woken him, that sixth sense, sharp as the other five in those who lived out in the wilds of the land. The Kiowa frowned, his eyes darting around the little campsite. He'd have the others awake in a second and Fargo's finger tightened on the trigger of the Spencer.

The rifle fired, sounded like a cannonshot in the quiet of the timberland. The Indian fell back onto the ground as though he'd been yanked by invisible strings. Fargo fired the Sharps instantly. The second Kiowa seemed as though he were tossing and turning in his sleep. Fargo scooped the Colt into his hand and fired. The others were leaping to their feet. He took the two closest together, blasted off two shots. The one Kiowa had started to run and his steps collapsed as he ran and he appeared to be growing smaller until he sank to the ground. The other brave had whirled, picked up his bow. Fargo's shot hit the bow, cutting it in half and slamming into the Indian's left side. The man spun around, turned back, his mouth hanging open. One half of him was bronze, the other drenched in scarlet.

Fargo didn't wait to watch him sink to the ground. He fired another shot at the fifth buck and missed as the Indian dived into the brush nearby. The one with the headband had also managed to take cover, Fargo saw with his mouth a thin, tight line. But he had cut the odds by two-thirds and the remaining two had no guns. He was satisfied but he knew better than to congratulate himself until it was over. He saw Bonnie's eyes peering into the trees, trying to find him, and the fear was still in them. He moved back a few paces, picked up the rifles, drew them back with him. He laid the Spencer on the ground beside a tree and held on to the Sharps as he slowly scanned the brush. He'd have no edge on stealth or patience, not as he had with most whites, and certainly none on hunting. He pushed back a little deeper into the brush and noted the grayness starting to creep into the woods. It didn't make him happy. Night would bring him no advantage now.

He stayed motionless, suddenly felt the tension take hold of him, the hairs on his arms stiffening. The odor drifted into his nostrils, the faintly musky smell of damp beaverskin. He uttered an oath as he dived flat and the bone knife slammed into the tree trunk just over his head to stick there, the handle quivering. He spun onto his back and saw the Kiowa leaping out of the brush at him, the tomahawk in his hand. Fargo spun, rolled, without time to bring the rifle around and the Indian landed where he had lain. The Kiowa whirled without stopping, came at him with the tomahawk carving the air. Once again, there was no time to bring the rifle up into firing position and Fargo ducked the first blow, went backward. Using the rifle as a club, holding on to the barrel with both hands, he swung, caught the onrushing Kiowa across the midsection. The Indian stopped and his jaw dropped as the breath went out of him. He started to double over when Fargo brought the stock up sharp, cracked the Kiowa on the point of the jaw. The Indian's eyes crossed before they glazed and he sank down to the ground with his jaw hanging loose and to one side.

Fargo took the tomahawk from his hand, tossed it into the brush, dropped to one knee and halted the sound of his own heavy breathing to listen. He heard none of the sounds he listened for, only a distant jaybird and the faint scrape of Bonnie tugging at the ties that kept her bound to the tree. The Kiowa with the headband hadn't come to back up his man. He stayed waiting, watching. Fargo let his own breath return, drew his lips back in distaste as the grayness began to deepen in the woodland. He saw Bonnie through the trees, frustration in her face as the bonds refused to loosen and suddenly he knew what the last Kiowa waited for. The Indian waited for him to free Bonnie. He would wait patiently, confidently, as the fox waits by the hole he knews the rabbit must use.

Fargo's eyes narrowed in thought. He could try to crawl his way in a circle and find the Kiowa. But that could take hours, inching along the ground until he had circled the entire area. Yet perhaps it was the only way and he swore at how quickly the dusk grew deeper. He let his mind race on, search for other options. He pressed his lips tight finally. He could always try to circle if he had to, he decided. But he'd try something else, first. All he wanted to know was where the Kiowa lay in wait. He rose, backed away, staying low as he made a half-circle to where he'd left the Ovaro. He climbed into the saddle, put the rifle away and took out the Colt .45.

He sent the horse forward at a fast canter, dropped low in the saddle as he reached the spot where Bonnie was tied. He wheeled the horse in a tight circle, leaned low on the far side of him and maneuvered the Ovaro almost against Bonnie, left only enough room for him to slide to the ground between her and the horse. He used his throwing knife to cut the rope first, then worked on the stronger, tougher leather thongs, still keeping the horse tight against them as a shield. His eyes darted around the trees as he worked on the thongs, his body pressed against

160

Bonnie, the Ovaro's side leaning into his back. But nothing moved and he cursed silently. The Kiowa was wily. He hadn't let himself be rushed into shooting. He was waiting for them to go, to run for it. Fargo's mouth was a hard slit as he stayed against Bonnie, his eyes sweeping the trees again. They could walk beside the Ovaro, use the horse as a shield again, but which side? "Damn," he swore. If he picked the wrong side they'd not get across the clearing. It was a choice he didn't dare make and his eyes grew narrow.

He'd let the Kiowa make the choice. And he'd wager on it. He moved to the side. "I'm going to slide around to the other side of the tree," he said to Bonnie. "You get on the Ovaro, stay flat over the withers. Head him straight across to where we came. Walk him, don't run him. Walk him and stay flat."

He started to slip around the tree trunk as Bonnie pulled herself onto the horse. He watched as she flattened herself low across the horse's withers, used her hold on the reins to turn the animal and start him across the small clearing. Fargo's eyes swept furiously from one side of the trees to the other as the horse slowly moved over the ground. He was halfway to the far trees and the Kiowa hadn't moved yet but Fargo clung to the wager he'd made with himself. It was the Indian's choice now, to let the girl ride away, go free, unharmed, and wait for his chance at the man who had come after them or to stop her. The Kiowa was a hunter, the instincts born and bred into him, a hunter and a warrior. Fargo was betting he couldn't let the girl get away, that he couldn't sit by and watch her just walk away in front of him. It would go against everything that was part of him.

Fargo felt the furrow dig into his brow. Bonnie

was almost at the other side. Once in the trees she'd be gone, beyond bow range. His eyes swept the half circle of trees again and suddenly he glimpsed the brush move, a quick rustle of leaves along the far right. He had the Colt aimed at the spot as the Kiowa rose, arrow drawn back on the bowstring, the shaft aimed at Bonnie. Fargo fired twice, his first shot hitting the Indian's arm and he saw the bow fly into the air with its arrow, the Indian twisting away in pain. The second shot slammed into the back of his head and he catapulted forward, the front of his head going on without the back.

Fargo stepped from beside the tree. Bonnie had halted, turned the Ovaro and came toward him. He strode to where her horse had been tied, got the animal and handed the reins to her. "We'll ride most of the night," he growled. "Got to make up all the time we saved on your shortcut."

"We got unlucky. It was a good idea," she said stubbornly.

"Don't have any more," Fargo said as he sent the Ovaro into a fast trot. "Unless they concern bed," he tossed back at Bonnie as she hurried after him.

7

He rode hard for the next two days, allowed only enough time for a few hours rest each night. The mountain trail proved to be direct enough as it follwed down from the other side of the crest, but it also had too many hunting parties and Fargo swore silently at Bonnie each time they had to lie in hiding. Or perhaps not so silently—since he was sure she heard him, nonetheless. It was almost dusk on the second day when Bonnie pointed to the tall peak in front of them. "Elder Mountain," she said. "The cemetery's halfway around the other side."

He increased the pace, headed westerly and they were near Elder Mountain when he held up one hand, slowed, his eyes fastened on the ground. He pointed to a large collection of hoofprints. "That'd be them," he said and frowned. "I think they've taken on company."

"What do you mean?"

"I don't know but let's find out," he said, and spurred the Ovaro forward, keeping the horse at a walk now. The prints led up the lower part of the mountain and Bonnie's voice took on an edge of excitement.

"It's got to be them," she said. "These prints are heading directly for the cemetery."

"And there are definitely more of them," Fargo added. The rising land flattened out some and became more timbered. The dusk was almost gone when Fargo halted, listened, caught the faint sound of voices ahead. He dropped from the Ovaro and started forward on foot, leading the horse behind him; Bonnie followed suit. The knot of figures came into view and Fargo saw the sudden flicker of half a dozen lights. "It's them. They're lighting lanterns," he said.

"Why'd they wait till night?" Bonnie asked.

"Somebody might come this way by day and see them. They'll be awhile. They're going to dig up the whole cemetery. They don't know where he buried the money. Even if they find one box they'll have to keep on for the others." He moved closer as the figures began to walk into the small cemetery with the lanterns. "They hired extra diggers. Five of them. They'll need them to do it in one night."

"Five extra diggers and five more guns," Bonnie said.

"With the three hands they brought with them that makes twelve. We can't take on twelve guns."

"We can't just sit here and watch them get away with it. Not after everything that's happened."

He shrugged. "I'm fresh out of answers. We can wait till after they've got the money. They'll divide it up and pay off the hired guns. I'd guess they might go back to Brushville."

"Back there?" Bonnie frowned.

"Why not? We're dead, so far as they know. What's to stop them?"

"You mean go after them then?"

"We could do it. One by one."

She thought for a moment. "I'm afraid of it. What if they don't go back? What if they take off on their own separate ways? Maybe we could catch them and maybe not. Or maybe we'd catch only one or two. That's not enough for me."

He nodded agreement. It wasn't enough for him either and he stared at the cemetery in angry frustration. They had started to dig and the thud of shovels on earth drifted through the darkness. The lanterns gave them more than enough light and he watched two of the hired men dig up a casket. They pulled it out of the hole, ripped the top off with a crowbar and spilled the contents out. He saw the skeleton fall out, come apart. The men shook the box again but nothing else followed. They kicked the bones back into the hole and pushed the casket in after them.

"The ghouls. The stinking, rotten ghouls," he heard Bonnie hiss. He nodded again and his eyes found Mariel Counsil. She still wore the cape and she seemed to be directing the operation. "Monsters. And we can't stop them," Bonnie said despairingly. "I can't sit here and watch them dig up the whole cemetery, the stinking ghouls."

Fargo turned his glance at Bonnie as her words danced in his mind. "Ghouls," he echoed softly. "Maybe we can stop them. You said you knew most of the families who've used this little cemetery for generations."

"Yes," she said.

"Well, now, I don't think they'd take kindly to grave robbers digging up their loved ones, do you?" Fargo said.

"They'd kill them. They'd go wild," Bonnie said as her eyes widened.

"Then what are we waiting for? Let's go tell them." Fargo grinned.

Bonnie was in the saddle before he mounted the Ovaro. "The Kecklers are nearest," she said, "just down the bend a ways." She started forward and Fargo followed as she led the way around a slow bend, down past a small stream and he saw the house and barns loom up in the night, lamplight from the house windows. The man that opened the door was bull-necked, in overalls, and Fargo saw two younger versions of him looking on from inside the house.

"It's me, Mr. Keckler. Bonnie Akins," Bonnie said as the man stared at the two visitors. Fargo saw his eyes widen with delayed recognition.

"Bonnie. Well, bless my soul. Haven't seen you around in some while," he said.

"It's a long story," she said quickly. "This is my friend, Skye Fargo."

"We just passed near to your cemetery. There's a whole gang of grave robbers digging it up," Fargo said.

"What?" the man said.

"No doubt the same gang I heard about back in Owlseville," Fargo said. "They've been hitting cemeteries all the way from back east in Kansas to out here."

"Grave robbin'? Diggin' up our kin?" the man bellowed.

"Lots of folks are buried with their favorite gold watch or a valuable necklace. That's what they look for," Fargo said.

"Get your guns, boys," the man roared. "We got us some grave robbers to kill."

"Wait," Fargo said. "There's a good lot of them and you know they'll shoot it out. We're riding to tell other folks. We'll tell them to meet here at your place."

"We'll go fast, Mr. Keckler," Bonnie said. "You get ready and wait for the others."

"Hurry up. I'm not much for waitin' while my kin is being dug up," the man said. Bonnie wheeled her horse and galloped away and Fargo caught up to her, stayed a few paces behind. She halted at a ranch near the foot of the mountain—the Hollymans'—and told the same story. The Rudolphs were next and, working around the base of Elder Mountain, the Albertsons and the Mackals next in line. They'd stopped at ten places when she halted.

"Enough," she said. "They'll each be bringing at least three with them. Let's get back to the Kecklers." Fargo rode beside her as they made their way back to the first house. Most of the others were gathered already and only the Mackals were still coming.

"Let's go," Keckler said. "I'm not waitin' for anybody else."

Fargo pushed the pinto to the front of the crowd. "Quiet does it. When we get near, we go the rest of the way on foot," he said. "You don't want them to hear you, scatter and get away, do you?"

"You're damned right we don't," someone said, and Fargo waved the others to follow. Bonnie came up beside him.

"I wanted to put a bullet in at least one of them myself," she muttered.

"A bullet's a bullet," Fargo said. "I don't care whose it is so long as it does the paying."

"I guess so," Bonnie said, and he rode up the pathway toward the cemetery. He took the others into the timberland, halted when he caught the dim glow of the lanterns in the distance. He swung to the ground, saw the others do the same. They started forward, not waiting. No need for them to wait. They knew the way, he was sure. He moved to one side, Bonnie staying with him, held to the far edge of the others as they spread out, almost marched toward the cemetery. He could feel the anger rising into the air as if it were something tangible as the men neared the cemetery. He let his eyes go to the gravesite. They had some quarter of the ground dug up, caskets lying upended, some sticking up from holes where they'd been tossed back. He saw one pine box placed to the side.

"They found one," he whispered to Bonnie. The lanterns afforded enough light, illuminating the head-stones to make them cast long shadows across the ground. Accusing fingers of darkness, he reflected. His eyes went to the line of men to his left. Keckler glanced across at him and Fargo nodded, saw the row of rifles lift into position.

"Goddamn heathen devils," he heard the bull-necked man roar and saw those in the cemetery look up, freeze in motion in a moment of shocked surprise. The moment shattered in the thunderous barrage of rifle fire that poured into the cemetery. Fargo saw two of the hired guns go down, two lanterns blown apart, and he watched the mayor try to turn and flee. A hail of bullets slammed into him. He shuddered, halted, shuddered again and toppled into one of the opened graves.

"Neatness counts," Fargo muttered as he fired a shot from the Colt and saw another of the hired uns fall to lie draped over a headstone. "Rest in eace," he murmured.

The others in the cemetery were shooting back, aking cover, some jumping into opened graves, oth-rs flattening themselves behind the larger headstones. Ie saw Bonnie raise the Spencer, fire at a man rying to make himself small enough to hide behind low headstone. He screamed, clutched at his leg nd rolled from behind the headstone. A shot from he other side slammed into him and he lay still. omeone inside the cemetery was smart enough to hoot the rest of the lanterns out and the site was lunged into blackness. Fargo blinked, waited, let his yes adjust to the pale moonlight that prevented the lark from being total.

"Circle the cemetery," he said to the others. "Circle and shoot whatever comes out."

He heard Keckler growl orders to the others and vatched the men move among the trees, begin to ircle the site. Someone moved inside the cemetery, darting shape that leaped from an opened grave. volley of shots resounded and the shape screamed, oppled over a headstone and lay still. The others vere completing the far side of the circle, he could ee, settling down to watch and wait.

"There are a lot of gaps," Bonnie said to him. Some can sneak out and get away."

"Maybe. There won't be many," he said. "These oys are pretty sharp-eyed." As if in answer, another igure started to race for the trees in a crouch, div-ng behind a headstone, then trying for another. He never made the second one as three shots knocked im down like a shooting-gallery figure.

Silence settled over the scene as those inside lay rapped and those outside had only to wait. Fargo's

eyes strained as he slowly scanned the shadowe
shapes, mounds and headstones of the cemetery. H
gave up, finally. It was impossible to pick out anyon
Over an hour had gone by when a voice called out.

"You out there," it said. "You're making a terribl
mistake. This is Sheriff Coleman of Brushville.
brought these men here on official business."

Fargo glanced at Keckler, saw the man's bull nec
turn to look at him, sudden dubiousness in the man'
eyes.

"You say you're a sheriff? Throw out your badge,
Keckler called. Fargo watched and saw the badge sa
into the air from one of the opened graves, th
moonlight catching the silver of the metal. "By Go
that is a badge," he heard Keckler say.

"I don't know who you all are but I'm here o
official business," the sheriff called out again. "No
you all back off and let me out of here and we ca
talk about this."

Keckler's eyes went to Fargo again and Bonnie'
whisper was filled with fear. "The bastard," she hissed
"These are good people who obey the law and God
Tell them he's lying."

"He's not lying about being a sheriff," Fargo said
"They saw the badge." His mind raced. It was to
complicated to explain, too much to pass around th
circle of men now suddenly unsure. Coleman sense
he'd struck pay dirt and his voice came again. "You
men have made a terrible mistake. Don't make i
worse," he shouted.

Keckler's eyes were turned, as were the eyes of th
two men beside him. "You said they were grav
robbers."

"He's one of them," Fargo said. "He supplies them
the records and the cemeteries."

"They killed Carrie because she found out about hem," Bonnie said.

"I'll be damned," the man said, whispered to the thers nearest him.

"Watch," Fargo said. "When he hears my voice he's oing to come apart. He thinks he killed me." Fargo urned from the man, lifted his voice. "Coleman, it's ne, Fargo. You're done for, you lying sonofabitch," e called.

He heard the shock in the silence that followed. Fargo," the sheriff's voice came, suddenly hoarse. No, you're dead."

"Not yet," Fargo said.

"Goddamn you," the sheriff screamed. "I'll kill ou myself, you interferin' sonofabitch." Fargo saw he dark shape start to rise, fall back as a barrage of hots split the night. He sat back, pressed Bonnie's rm. His eyes lifted, sought the dim moon. It had anished behind the mountain.

"I'm tied of waitin'," he heard Keckler say. "I can't tand those bastards sitting in our kinfolks' places. 'm going to go in and wipe them out."

"It'll be dawn in a half hour," Fargo said. "You'll e able to do it from here then."

Keckler fell silent, his face dark with anger. The ninutes ticked away with sudden slowness and they roved too slow. Keckler rose suddenly, called out. argo saw the shapes rise around the perimeter of he cemetery. Keckler's shot was the trigger. The ight erupted in gunfire as the circle of men ran orward, firing as fast as they could into the cemetery. argo rose, started forward, fired at the darting shapes hat appeared inside the cemetery. Bonnie beside im, he moved closer but the gunfire had become vild, unorganized, a hail of bullets being pumped

171

into the cemetery as fast as the old rifles could be fired and reloaded. He halted, pulled Bonnie back with him, dropped to one knee. The gray light of the new day streaked the sky as the gunfire came to an end, the sharp smell of gunpowder floating through the air.

The row of figures stood at the edges of the cemetery in the new dawn light, peering in at the opened graves, the disarray of caskets and broken bone spilling out. "Anybody hurt?" he heard the bull necked man call out.

"Billy Mackal's hit in the leg. Tom Albertson's got an arm wound and Herbie Rudolph's got a crease rib," someone called back. Fargo rose, moved forward with Bonnie as the others stepped into the cemetery. His searching eyes spotted Coleman, first the man half out of one of the graves, his body riddled with holes. Fargo stepped carefully through the debris, glanced at the lifeless forms of the hired hands. He found the banker huddled behind headstone, his legs drawn up as though he were kneeling in prayer. Three bullet holes oozed red from his side and back. "We know the mayor's in one of the graves," Fargo said.

"That leaves her. She's not here," Bonnie said. "She got away last night. Somehow she sneaked through."

Fargo's eyes went to the far side of the cemetery. "She had to go that way," he said. "The circle had the biggest holes at that point." He turned, started to walk back across the graveyard. "I'll get her. You stay here. You've friends among these people. I might be back soon and I might not."

Bonnie said nothing and he felt her eyes watch him as he retrieved the Ovaro, rode around the cemetery to the far side. He saw her watch him as he dismounted, searched the ground carefully, painstakingly. The underbrush made finding marks hard, most of those he found were the flat prints of boots. But he continued to scan the forest floor and he halted suddenly, the small, sharp imprint of a woman's heel in the soil. He followed, saw the others, swung onto the Ovaro and picked up the trail. She hadn't been gone long, he saw, the marks freshly dug in. She must have left only minutes before the barrage began. He kept the horse at a slow walk, frowned as the marks continued in a straight line, unhurried, as though made by someone out on a stroll.

He moved past a heavy, gnarled oak and saw the flat rock beyond it. The figure sat there, the cape around her shoulders, eyes on him as he approached. Mariel Counsil stood as he reached her, a tiny smile playing on her lips. "I expected you," she said. "When you called out to Coleman I knew there'd be no getting away from you. I managed to leave there then. I wanted our last meeting to be just between us." She studied his handsomely chiseled face, now as if carved in stone. "I'm amazed, though, I must admit. No one has ever gotten away from Treeman."

"It wasn't easy," he said flatly.

"Are you going to kill me now?" Mariel asked.

"I'd like to," he said. "But then it might be more fitting to see you hung."

"The others are busy trying to put their little cemetery in order, I take it," she said.

"That's right. You walk back in front of me."

The little smile came again. "Not yet." She drew her arms from under the cape. He found himself staring into the barrel of a heavy Walker Colt. "You see, I waited for you because I knew I'd be at a

173

disadvantage if I let you hunt me down. Now I can be rid of you once and for all. Drop your gun belt. I'd rather we walk a little further on before I shoot you. I don't want anyone hearing and running after you."

Fargo eyed the Walker. It was held steady as a rock. He unbuckled his gun belt and let it drop. Mariel Counsil wouldn't hesitate to put a bullet through him a few minutes earlier than she'd planned. He stepped away from the gun on the ground and the Walker followed him without a waver. "You seem quite unstoppable, Fargo," she said. "But it's time we put an end to that."

"I don't think so," the voice said, and Fargo spun to see Bonnie step from around the big oak, the Spencer in her hands, pointed at Mariel Counsil. Surprise came into the woman's eyes but she kept the Walker on the big man.

"The fair damsel to the rescue," she slid out.

"No, I followed him because I want you, all for myself," Bonnie said, and Fargo saw the rage deep in the brown eyes, a fire that blazed with the intensity of pain and anguish and the cry for justice.

Mariel Counsil's smile widened a fraction. "I'm afraid you'll not have that pleasure, any more than he will," she said.

"Drop the gun or I'll kill you," Bonnie said.

"You shoot and I pull this trigger. You may kill me but your good friend here will be as dead as I am," the woman answered. Fargo gauged the distance to the gun, decided it would be certain suicide. "You shoot and I shoot, simple as that. You can make it a double funeral," the woman said. Her cold smile stayed as she flicked her eyes from Fargo to

Bonnie. "You don't want that, do you?" she said to the girl.

"Kind of a Mexican stand-off, I guess," Bonnie said.

"It needn't be. We can make a deal," the woman said. "You put that rifle down and I'll let him live. You both agree not to come after me, now or ever." She paused, her eyes going back and forth. "No deal and he's a dead man. You see, I've nothing to lose now."

"What about your pistol?" Bonnie asked.

"I'll put it down too. If I have your word." Her eyes stayed on Bonnie a moment longer, flicked to Fargo. "Is it a deal?" she asked, her eyes returning to Bonnie. "Not that you've much choice," she added. Bonnie nodded. "You'll stick to it?" the woman pressed.

"Of course," Bonnie said. "You've my word."

Mariel Counsil's eyes went to Fargo. "I want to hear you say it," she demanded.

"Bonnie's agreed. I won't break her word," Fargo said.

The woman's smile was malevolently triumphant. "Good. A reasonable decision," she said, waited, watched Bonnie start to lower the rifle. Bonnie halted, watched and waited also. The woman bent down, put the Walker Colt on the ground, almost with a flourish, certain of her knowledge of human nature. She started to turn away, saw Bonnie raise the Spencer. She dived for the pistol but it was too late. The Spencer roared and Mariel Counsil clutched her abdomen, fell backward.

Fargo stared at Bonnie, watched her walk up to Mariel Counstil. The woman's eyes looked up at her, disbelief in their pale tan depths, disbelief and a last rage. "Bitch. Lying, rotten bitch," Mariel Counsil hissed.

"Fool. Stupid fool. I'm a quick learn, remember?" Bonnie flung back, spun away and stood trembling, her fists clenched. Mariel Counsil tried another epithet but her last breath failed her. Fargo pryed Bonnie's hands from the rifle, held her with one arm as he walked back to the Ovaro.

"I've never broken my word before," Bonnie said to him.

"You couldn't have picked a better time."

"Was I wrong, Fargo?" she asked, little-girl-like.

"A tooth for a tooth," he said. "as you put it, you're a quick learn."

She clung to him. "Take me somewhere, Fargo. Make me forget all of it."

"Can't make you forget. I can just make you not remember for a little while," he told her.

"That'll do," she said. "That'll do just fine."

He nodded, remembering the sweet passion of her lovemaking. It would definitely do just fine.

LOOKING FORWARD

**The following is the opening section
from the next novel in the exciting
Trailsman series from Signet:**

The Trailsman #25
MAVERICK MAIDEN

*A sizzling summer in early Texas, when the guns in the
territory turned as hot as hell itself . . .*

Fargo scuttled over the sharp, jagged rock to the
smooth shoulder high on the side of the gorge. From
here he could see the top of the grizzled rocks, and
his gun was out, ready to blow the head off this
mystery, mangy, sneaky gunman who'd been trying
to potshot him for the last two days. He shot always
from high ground and then moved like greased
lightning. By the time Fargo made the climb, his
target skidded into thin air—like now.

The sun on this side of the gorge hit down like a
hammer, and Fargo mopped the sweat off his bronzed
square face. His piercing lake-blue eyes raked every
inch of the rocks, searching for a move, while his
ears strained for sound.

Suddenly an alarm did go off, for he heard sound,
but it came not from the gorge but from the canyon.
Two men were on horses, skulking behind the boul-
ders that bordered the trail. They were waiting, and

from Fargo's perch, he could see clearly enough what they waited for—a short-haul Texas wagon with its driver and four passengers running easy for Eagle Butte. Running, Fargo thought, right into ambush.

Fargo felt a jolt of anger at the cards being dealt him. First, he was trying to get to Red Clay to track down a lead in his quest for revenge. Second, he'd been sidetracked by this mystery bushwhacker who, for no damned logical reason, had been throwing lead at him. Now he was about to be pushed into the crossfire of a trailway robbery.

He gritted his teeth, and for a closer look at the gunmen, moved with catlike step down over the scarred iron-colored rocks. Now he had a sharper view and he stared hard at the two men, now with guns drawn. They were both stubble-bearded, short, muscular, with the same body stamp, except one was a bit leaner, taller. They wore black hats, black vests, red kerchiefs. As Fargo studied them, the short one spoke and the lean one laughed, an ugly hard laugh. The kind of laugh that triggered a memory of men he often seemed to meet in the territory, men of evil. He thought of his dead family and felt a surge of hate and moved down, quiet and fast. The gunmen were unaware of him, but on the other hand, they were out of his rifle range. To be helpful to the passengers in that wagon, he knew he should get into the action plenty fast. It was a Texas cotton-bed wagon, with its top sawed off, used for short hauls.

He shot a glance at the driver, big-shouldered, big hat, riding easy, blissfully ignorant that behind the curve in the trail he was headed right into a trap. Fargo felt his breathing come quicker and cursed softly. Then, as the driver slowed his team because of the curve, the two gunmen moved out, blocking the trail. Startled at the sight ahead of him, the driver pulled hard on the reins and the horses came to a halt, snorting and stomping.

"What the hell," the driver said, slowly raising his hands.

The short man shot him anyway, quickly, as if the idea had already been in his head. The big driver grabbed at his chest, then cursed as he pitched face down to the ground.

Fargo's jaw hardened and he measured the distance—still out of range. He moved faster, silently, from boulder to boulder. He had an ugly foreboding.

The gunmen swung off their horses with guns pointing and yelled hard at the passengers. They came down slowly, two portly men in vested suits, a dude in black Eastern suit, a buxom, brown-haired girl in a blue cotton dress. They looked at the bleeding body of the driver, then stared in fear at the gunmen.

"Throw your money here," the short man yelled, waving his gun, while the lean gunman bit into a wad of tobacco. The portly men hurriedly pulled their wallets and tossed them. The dude was scowling, his pale face twisted with disbelief—he couldn't understand the violence. "Are you men crazy? You can't get away with this!"

The lean man had bent to pick up a wallet, but at the words he froze, then shot the dude in the heart. The bullet flung him back as if he'd been hit by a hammer and he sat down, his eyes like saucers, staring. Slowly he put his hand to his bloody chest, stared at it, amazed, looked at the gunman, then slid down to the earth.

The short man glared at the lean man, shook his head. "That was stupid, Luke. Now we gotta be mean." And he shot the other two men and, when they fell squirming to the ground, he shot them again.

Fargo cursed; it had been too quick, and he had made a mistake. If he had fired, even if his bullets fell short, it might have saved the men by distracting the gunmen.

These were killers without mercy, he hadn't expected that. They had killed to eliminate witnesses, and now he feared for the girl. After they pleasured themselves with her, there'd be no telling what might happen. He had to move fast.

The girl, horrified by the killings, panicked and began to run. "Grab her, Shorty," Luke smirked. Shorty laughed, made a sprinting tackle and brought her down. As he rolled over her, contact with her body seemed to trigger his desires, and he began to pull at her dress. A rip brought out her breasts and the sight of them made him whistle.

"Hey, Luke," he called," Lookit this piece. Ever see such tits?"

Luke's mind seemed to be on money, for he kept picking the pockets of the men and looking into the wallets.

Shorty tried to get the girl's dress up, but she fought him, and furious, her ripped it completely off her body, pulling and tearing until she was absolutely nude. "Hey, Luke, forget the money. Look at this. It's cherry, I'll bet, the best there is."

The girl had full breasts, full hips, a wellshaped body. She squirmed so hard that Shorty, who had opened his breeches, couldn't make headway. "C'mere Luke, hold her hands," he yelled. "I'm going to nail this hellcat."

Luke came over, and by this time, Fargo felt he had picked up range. Maybe it's been a good idea anyway to wait until the men were near each other. Luke had grabbed the girl's hands, and Shorty was trying to get between the girl's thighs, but she squirmed and twisted, and Shorty, in a fury of frustration, swung at the girl, knocking her flat. He stood and looked at her, scowling. For a moment she lay stunned, then slowly got up and faced him, a red bruise on her cheek.

Shorty took his gun from its holster, unbuttoned his belt, let his breeches drop to his ankles. His organ was in a state of real excitement. Deliberately he shot a bullet at her feet, raising dust. "I'm tired of rassling you, you lil' bitch. Now I'll give you just one minute to come over here and make love to this thing or I'll put a bullet in your bush."

The words floated clearly up to Fargo and his face reddened with anger.

The girl looked at Shorty's erection with revulsion, and though in fear, she lifted her head. "Shoot, you skunk, because I'd rather die."

Shorty, his face hard, threatening, slowly raised his gun.

Now Fargo had him in sight and squeezed the trigger. Shorty shrieked and looked down. Only a bleeding stump was left of his penis. He shrieked again and again in pain, in anguish, in horror.

Luke stared at him in shock, then pulled his gun,

searching for the gunman in the high rocks, but the next bullet hit his own right eye, blasting it, and with it, part of his skull. He fell like an axed tree.

The girl looked as if a thunderbolt from heaven had saved her, and her eyes, scanning the rocks, saw the lean, square-faced man with the rifle now coming toward her.

Shorty was staring at Luke, then looked down to see the blood of his life pumping out of his groin. He fell to his knees, his face grimacing horribly, and struggled to raise his gun to fire at the lean rifleman coming toward him. The rifle shot echoed in the gorge and a hole appeared in Shorty's head as his brains spurted into the air and he fell forward, face down.

The girl screamed, covered her eyes, grabbed her clothing and ran behind a rock.

"Nothing more to worry about, miss," Fargo said quietly.

He looked down at Luke, who was not a pretty sight, his pockets bulging with stolen wallets. "No point in wasting this," he said. He put the booty all together into a red neckerchief and then looked at the young woman coming from behind the rock. The rips in the dress she wore still revealed parts of her body. She was a pretty thing, he thought, a pert face, dark-brown eyes, a sweet mouth, and she was certainly gutsy.

"They were no gentlemen," his voice was ironic.

"They were animals . . . worse!" She bit her lip. "I don't know how to thank you."

He stared at the men so quiet in death, their evil brought to a violent standstill. "Don't thank me. It's a pleasure to wipe such men from the face of the earth." He turned. "Where you headed, miss?"

"My name is Amy Jackson. I was headed for Eagle Butte."

"Just get up on that black horse, Miss Jackson. I'll give you escort."

A quiver of anxiety flashed in her face, as if she were wondering if he were a man to be trusted. He'd seen her naked, after all. Fargo understood her concern. "My name is Skye Fargo. I don't think you need worry too much from now on."

He sounded right, and suddenly reassured, she flashed him a look of gratitude and swung over the black's saddle.

When they reached Eagle Butte, a small worried group had collected at the depot with its painted sign: Clem Barker's Short-Haul Line. A gray-haired, pink-faced lady in the group waved at sight of Amy. The others looked shocked as they observed the state of her clothes, the bruise on her face.

"My God, Amy, what happened?" the lady cried.

Amy dismounted and they crowded around while the girl told the details, not sparing any of the horror of the holdup and massacre, and particularly Fargo's sharpshooting.

The listeners were shocked at the brutal killings. "It was those mean Jones boys," a hard-faced cowboy said. One heavy-set man in a brown Stetson stared with hostile eyes at Fargo. "Why didn't you shoot the moment you saw the holdup, mister? Why'd you wait?"

Fargo grimaced. "I was out of range. And thought

it'd just be a robbery, that I'd have time. Not often men kill so easy for money."

"These men do," said the cowboy. "The Jones boys, Shorty and Luke. Wanted for killings all over the territory."

Fargo stroked his cheek. "I suppose I should have fired, even out of range. It might have stopped them. It was a mistake."

"You made a mistake, mister, and my cousin is dead," said the heavy-set man.

"It's very sad that you lost your cousin, Clem," said Mrs. Jackson. "But the killers are dead. And Amy is alive and unhurt because of Mr. Fargo. I think instead of blaming him, we owe him thanks."

The other people nodded, and one man grunted. "Got rid of two of the worst killers in the county."

Fargo nodded and smiled at Amy who flashed him a warm, grateful look. He walked down the dirt street lined with white or unpainted wooden buildings: a livery shop, a general merchandise store, Mama Joy's Cafe, a saloon and Brown's Hotel. Two crusty buildings that looked abandoned brought up the end of the street.

Fargo took a room at the hotel for the night, washed his grimy face in a basin of hot water, sprawled on the bed for an hour, joying in its soft luxury. Then he went out, down the street and toward Miller's Saloon.

The saloon was surprisingly big, a long bar, with a mirror behind it, several drinkers, two tables with card players, and a battered piano played by a sad-faced black man. Three women in low-cut red dresses and spangled jewelry, laughing, were in the back, near stairs that obviously went up to private rooms.

The barman, Miller, came up, a man with a red face, big red nose, shrewd brown eyes.

"Whiskey," Fargo said.

The barman poured a drink, studied Fargo a moment, then smiled. He set up another glass, filled it. "Have one on the house, mister," he smiled.

"Why?"

"You're Fargo, right? We heard about the stage-coach. And we heard too about Shorty Jones. What you did." He grinned. "You shortened him a bit, I heard. And you shot from up in the hills. Must have an eye like an eagle."

Fargo picked up his glass. "Thanks for the drink." When the barman went off to attend another customer, Fargo looked into the mirror. He could see the women clearly enough and found it pleasing to look at one of them, a redhead with a pretty face, surprisingly abundant breasts in a slender, well-shaped body. She wore a red silk-like dress, tight against her figure, its lowcut showing a fine pair of deep breasts. She couldn't be more than twenty, and her face had the kind of innocence that would always be there, whatever way she lived. She seemed busy laughing at a story told by one of the women. Just then one of the men from the bar came over, bent low and whispered in her ear; whatever it was, it hit her hard, for she turned sharply to look right at the reflection in the mirror. With the quickness of a clever woman, she zeroed in on Fargo's interest, smiled brightly. Then she walked to an empty table, sat down, and crooked her finger at him, which made him smile.

She had no doubt that he'd come over. She was a damned pretty thing, and could fascinate any man who appealed to her, and, for one moment, he was tempted to throw a block, stay put, and see how she handled it. Then decided against it. He hadn't had a woman for weeks, and his groin was in an uproar, specially after the sight of Amy, all nude and luscious out on the trail. He couldn't very well tackle Amy after her scary experience with the Jones boys, but this girl, bold, deep-chested, young for a party girl, looked irresistible to him. So he took his glass and ambled over to her table.

For some reason, the pianist at that moment decided to play, and it was a romantic, pretty tune that sounded just fine for his intentions.

"Did you invite me?" he asked.

"Oh yes. You are Fargo, aren't you?"

He nodded, surprised, and sat down. Close up, she had a fine acquiline nose, a wide-lipped mouth and gray eyes. Her red hair curled pleasingly around her face, which had a few freckles, and the white bulge of her breasts made him feel hornier than ever.

"I'm Fargo."

"I'm Mady," she said. "And I want to thank you for ridding the world of a sewer rat."

His eyebrows went up. "Who would that be?"

"Shorty Jones, that's who it would be." Her eyes flashed fire. "The rottenest rat that ever lived."

He lifted his glass. "It sounds personal."

"It's personal, all right!" Her eyes suddenly filled with tears. "He shot and killed my father two years ago. In Glen Rose, where we had a general store.

186

Came in one day for bullets, he was all out. When my father asked for money, he said, "You got it all wrong, mister. It's you who pays the money. And he pointed the gun at dad. 'That's a lowdown trick,' dad says. I was in the store at the time. 'I'm sorry you don't like my manners,' said Shorty, 'but I don't like to be cussed.' Then he shot daddy, just like that, two bullets. Paralyzed him. Then Shorty grabbed the money in the drawer, said he was sorry he didn't have time for me just then, and raced off, to his brother, standing watch outside. These Jones boys were the worst in the territory. And I heard the way you did Shorty in. Everyone in town's heard it. We ought to give you a medal." She leaned forward, put her soft fingers on his face, and planted a warm kiss on his lips.

He grinned, pulled a cheroot, scratched the match on his jeans. "I'm glad to avenge your daddy. The truth is, I hate scum like that wherever I see it. And I try to do my bit to clean up the territory, if I can."

She was looking at his dusty clothes. "You been riding long, haven't you? Where you headed?"

"Trying to nail two more sewer rats."

"If you're not in a hurry, maybe you could stop for a bath." Her eyes fixed on his, and her full lips smiled meaningly. "You might want to ease up some. A man needs to ease up."

He felt a hardening in his breeches, and Mady, with the instinct of a woman who knew when such things happen, suddenly smile.

He followed her upstairs to a spacious room that looked very feminine, with frilly curtains on the window, a cloth on the bureau, a red coverlet on the large bed. He sat on the bed testing its softness. "This feels good," he said.

She was standing in front of him, a full-fleshed woman with all her curves in the right places. Her breasts pushed tightly against her red dress, which gleamed in the yellow light of the lamp. He could see the imprint of her nipples against the silk, and a scent of perfume floated from her body. Her gray eyes seemed to glow, as if with anticipation of excitement to come. His own body was already in a rage of hunger, and his britches were bristling with the shape of it. It was not a thing that would escape the practiced eye of a woman like her, and she smiled, aware of her power. Her breasts in front of him were irresistibly tempting, and he slipped his finger under her dress, eased out one breast, strikingly white, its nipple pink and erect with passion. He put his lips to it, flicked his tongue at the nipple, put his hand over her shapely butt. He stroked her body, lifted her dress, and unsurprisingly she wore only a silky chemise underneath so that he touched the velvety skin of her butt. He brought his hand around to the front, stroked her soft mound, then parted the erotic crease, bringing his finger to the moist warmth within. He stroked her like this for a few minutes, and then with a sigh, she kneeled, worked quickly to open his britches, brought out his ponderous potency, and with a quick movement took his fullness into her mouth. She moved deftly, deliberately, with intense hunger. She was daring in the movement of her lips and tongue, so that his pleasure sharpened, and the urgency of his desire made him withdraw abruptly. He quickly pulled down his jeans, while she, also caught by passion, flung her clothes aside. Her body was voluptuous, a high waist, full hips, shapely thighs and fleecy maidenhair over the erotic triangle. She slipped onto the bed, her rounded arms out, her thighs apart, looking on his bristling excitement. He put his body against the warmth of her flesh, caressed the silk of her skin, and she brought him to the lush warm opening. He slid deep into her, felt the marvelous soft flesh surround him, and began to move. He kept firm control, and several times during his thrusting her body tightened, and she groaned as if her pleasure had pain in it. Then, feeling the rising surge, he began strong powerful thrusts that made her clench her teeth to keep from screeching, and then he felt himself swell to bigness and suddenly surge into her. It made her go wild and her body twisted this way and that, as if the feeling was too much to bear. They lay this way for a long time, coming down from a high way up.

After a while, they did it all over again.

JOIN THE <u>TRAILSMAN</u> READER'S PANEL
AND PREVIEW NEW BOOKS

If you're a reader of <u>TRAILSMAN</u>, New American Library wants to bring you more of the type of books you enjoy. For this reason we're asking you to join <u>TRAILSMAN</u> Reader's Panel, to preview new books, so we can learn more about your reading tastes.

Please fill out and mail today. Your comments are appreciated.

1. The title of the last paperback book I bought was:_____

2. How many paperback books have you bought for yourself in the last six months?
☐ 1 to 3   ☐ 4 to 6   ☐ 10 to 20   ☐ 21 or more

3. What other paperback fiction have you read in the past six months? Please list titles:_____
_____
_____
_____

4. I usually buy my books at: (Check One or more)
☐ Book Store   ☐ Newsstand   ☐ Discount Store
☐ Supermarket   ☐ Drug Store   ☐ Department Store
☐ Other (Please specify)_____

5. I listen to radio regularly: (Check One)   ☐ Yes   ☐ No
My favorite station is:_____
I usually listen to radio (Circle One or more)   On way to work /
During the day / Coming home from work / In the evening

6. I read magazines regularly: (Check One)   ☐ Yes   ☐ No
My favorite magazine is:_____

7. I read a newspaper regularly: (Check One)   ☐ Yes   ☐ No
My favorite newspaper is:_____
My favorite section of the newspaper is:_____

For our records, we need this information from all our Reader's Panel Members.
NAME:_____
ADDRESS:_____
TELEPHONE: Area Code (   ) Number_____   ZIP_____

8. (Check One)   ☐ Male   ☐ Female

9. Age (Check One)   ☐ 17 and under   ☐ 18 to 34
☐ 35 to 49   ☐ 50 to 64   ☐ 65 and over

10. Education (Check One)
☐ Now in high school   ☐ Graduated high school
☐ Now in college   ☐ Completed some college
☐ Graduated college

As our special thanks to all members of our Reader's Panel, we'll send a free gift of special interest to readers of THE TRAILSMAN.

Thank you. Please mail this in today.

NEW AMERICAN LIBRARY
PROMOTION DEPARTMENT
1633 BROADWAY
NEW YORK, NY 10019

Exciting Westerns by Jon Sharpe from SIGNET

SIGNET Westerns You'll Enjoy